CheckMate

IT'S YOUR MOVE

CheckMate

It's Your Move

By: Lex
Copyright © 2015

ISBN: 978-0-9996746-1-1
Library of Congress Control Number: 2017963341

Copyright Registration:
TX001964552 2015-04-18

Published by:
The Solid Foundation Group, LLC
www.TheSolidFoundationGroup.com

Printed in the United States of America

ACKNOWLEDGEMENTS

I would love to give great acknowledgement to my parents, Leetha Day and Otis Day, for bringing me into existence, for without them I could not manifest any of my ideas or thoughts; my brother, Damien Day, and sister, Ebonique Day aka Lady Picasso aka LaSilk aka Twin - for your support.

A must needed shout-out to the blissful and inspiring couple I know: Kwame J. and Monyia Essence at Copper Vibrations and Read1Write1. Thanks for the support, book cover, good vibes, and food (lol).

To my extended family that I've known since my days of incarceration to now, we gonna make it. My Day, Fye, Pitt, family geesh too many to name y'all know who y'all are. To Motivations Barber Shop for allowing me to refurnish my life again after years of being away. To my co-worker, Torris Johnson, who put that drive back in me to get the ball rolling on this project. You already know I got plenty more bullets in the chamber. Oh man, I have to say this before he gets mad at me, this my right-hand man more than a friend but family: PD, u already know, bro...nothing but love this way. We doing it, bro.

Last thanks to The Solid Foundation Group for publishing my work. Get ready...I'm coming with more.

PROLOGUE

Life. What is life? Life is like a game of chess. The only exception is that once you lose your life you can't start over, rewind or play it again. How you survive and make it in life is determined by your very first move: the opening move. This tells your opponent what kind of thinker you are. It takes logic, tolerance, and patience to win at this game. Without these things you're just another nobody watching things happen instead of making things happen. The key to this game is to know and understand each move you make and the consequences behind them.

At times you have to think two to three moves ahead because one move can achieve the same thing as three if done right. The game consists of you, the king. You can only move on space in any direction. You're weak and vulnerable, but the most important on the board. Why? Because you're the mastermind, and without a brain the body can't function. So, you build an army.

The Queen, your girl, wifey, that ride or die chick. She's the most powerful piece on the board, going places that you're not allowed just to get info, stray a few people, kill or seduce your opponent's king. The Bishops, your captains, control the territory and make sure everything runs smoothly. This could be your right-hand man, best friend or whoever. The knight is your executioner the lieutenant, who makes sure all things are done correctly. The rooks protect your fortress, your foundation. They make sure nothing less than an army can penetrate your walls. Then you have your pawns. These are some powerful pieces, because they know that they're weak, but continue trying to make a point.

They'll sacrifice their life for their king with no hesitation. Some pawns come back as power players and help those who kept it real with them.

The object of the game is to gain control of your opposition and hold a steady position. Any and every mistake can result in three things. Check, stalemate, or checkmate. Check can come at you in several ways. Where you might have to go on the run, you might catch beef and end up losing out or giving something up. Stalemate is when you're put in a position where you can't go anywhere like prison. Then there's checkmate, death. If you play it smart your game will improve and you'll be ready to challenge anybody. But everybody doesn't think the same. Sacrifices have to be made. Will you give up your Queen in order to keep fighting or those pawns who look up to you, trying to prove their loyalty? Will your choices lead you to a steady flow of victories or will your game end before any goals are accomplished? Decisions, decisions. Some are hard, some are easy, but for some, it was all about survival.

PART I - PICK YOUR PIECES

CHAPTER 1

Solomon "Solo" Divine's whole life was dedicated to the streets, it was all he knew. He stood at five seven with a solid build. The cornrows that covered his head, touched the top of his shoulders, where you could see how the sun darkened his complexion. He was born in the revolutionary era of Afros, leather jackets, dashikis, and black fists. But grew up through the dookie ropes, troops, kangos and gazelles into the crack epidemic, Old English and eight ball jackets. His perception was that 'if he couldn't do it, it couldn't be done.'

He was an intelligent person. He was what they called the best of both worlds, streetwise plus book smart. In the past five years he lost himself in every book that he could get a hold of. From religion, to self-knowledge, to books on revolution. Even books that broadened his thinking of women. Thanks to Sharazad Ali. It was a must to know about authors and people such as Na'im Akbar, Ralph Epperson, Dr. York, Elijah Muhammad, Malcolm X, Clarence 13x, George Jackson, Eldridge Clever, Assata Shakur, Marcus Garvey and such.

When he wasn't reading or making moves, he played chess. He learned the game from his brother Shakim, who was almost a Grand Master. At first he didn't like the game, because he couldn't win. Now, after many years of sharpening his skills he loved the game, He didn't play against people unless they were a challenge. So he usually played against himself, waiting for the day to go head up with his brother. He knew that besides him, no one was a bigger challenge than the man he had to look at in the mirror every day. It got to the point that he started seeing life like a game of chess. He became the pieces and every move was like a step in his already twisted world. You couldn't lose focus or you'd lose the game. But the game he was about to begin was a serious matter. He was a two-time felon and had no more room for mistakes.

Solo lay on his bed, hand in his pants and arm covering his eyes. This was an everyday thing, laying like this, as he formed a mental board in his head and placed the pieces in their proper place. He had been playing this game for a little over a year now. This time there was no starting over or re-evaluating. He would have to play this one out until one of the two things happened: Victory or Death.

As he thought about his opening move, he heard his room door open. What stood there was something he would be looking at for the very last time.

"Divine, you ready?" the female correctional officer, who stood like an Amazon in the doorway asked.

"Yeah, I'm ready." Solo answered while placing his feet on the floor and grabbing his bags of personal belonging.

The guard placed a piece of paper in his pocket and gave him a peck on the cheek. "Make sure you call me."

"You know I am," he replied.

Jordan East had held him down for the last couple of years, on the weed tip. She also helped relieve his sexual tensions. She was all right but not for him. He knew that once he walked through those gates, he was leaving everything behind, even her.

It was 8:15 in the morning when he stepped out of the DOC car and onto the Greyhound. At the same time he placed his king down on its square.

CHAPTER 2

The bus ride he took was like one of those experiences you wished you could escape but had to wait out. Solo sat staring out the window trying to ignore the man sitting beside him, who was busting his eardrums about how he had just did an eleven year bid. He was headed back to the city of Greensboro, home of the A&T Aggies and the all-girl Bennett College. Even though he saw first hand as the signs and exits passed before his eyes, it took a lot for him not to think of it as just another one of his dreams.

He wondered how it would feel to walk and talk freely. To have your rights back. Even though you couldn't tell by looking at him, the excitement was there. It was just that he knew how to hide his emotions, because when you dealt with emotions you tended to do things unconsciously. Just as happy as he was to be free, he was equally as sad. There was nothing much to come home to. His mother had died from an overdose of pills she took for her depression. He never understood what stressed her out enough to cause her to do what she did. He always thought of her as a strong woman. To raise him, she had to be. It probably came from being unemployed, lonely and losing her eldest son, that drove her to it.

All he had left now was his grandmother, Miss Rose. She was respected throughout her neighborhood. Probably because of her pure Indian heritage and the fact that they thought that she would put a root on them. His generation was backwards. Too many elders were burying their young instead of the other way around. Solo lost a lot throughout his life, but he wouldn't allow old wounds to bust back open. He learned to turn his pain into strength and prosper with it.

Miss Rose was seventy-two years old, but looked to be fifty-two. The only exception was the silver hair that came down to the top of her butt in one long plait. She became the mother that he needed. All of his certificates, diplomas and pictures went to her. The Mother's Day cards with portraits he had other prisoners draw, were all for her. Through his entire sentence, she was the one who kept his head from bowing and giving up hope. He couldn't wait to see her.

As he stepped off the bus with his bag in one hand and a $45 gateway check in the other, he stopped to take a gulp of air from the free world. The only thing was, that he didn't know how he wanted to go home. He didn't know where to cash his check, but that didn't matter, because he was standing on five hundred dollars cash that he made before his release. Since he couldn't do it before, he decided to walk home.

As he made his way down Gate City Blvd. he began reciting the Azan, the Islamic call to prayer. He felt his spirits lift with every word. No one seemed to pay him no mind, nor did it seem like anyone recognized him. He didn't care because he didn't plan on messing with any of these cats anyway.

When he got to his grandma's house, no one was home. He made his way onto the back porch and through the sliding glass door that stayed unlocked. After putting down his stuff, he went to the kitchen and pulled out a bottle of spring water. Just as he was turning away from the refrigerator he felt cold steel at the base of his neck.

"Make one move and I'm taking ya whole head off," Miss Rose said from behind him.

Solo turned to look at his grandma and seen her clutching a ten-gauge pump. "Grandma, it's me."

"Me who?"

"Solo."

"Solo? Boy when you get out?" she asked lowering the shotgun.

"I got out this morning."

"How, you escape or something?"

"Naw, I told you my lawyer said my appeal had come through."

"Boy, I thought you were bullshitting. Come here and give ya grandma a hug."
Solo walked towards her and engulfed her in his massive arms. "My baby's finally home," Miss Rose said rocking him back and forth in her arms.

Pulling away she looked him up and down. "Look at my boy all big and strong. You gonna have these girls chasing you all over the place."

"Go 'head now."

"Don't go head me. I know you ain't had you none in a while. I know how it is, I was young once too you know. You get all tensed up. That's what's probably wrong wit people now. They ain't getting enough, got too much energy."

"Damn, grandma, what done got into you?"

"Ain't nothing got into me. I'm just telling the truth. And another thing. You better put on some protection, cause as bad as I want some grandkids, I don't want any ol' type like your sister done popped out. Matter fact let me call your sister, she running around in my car like it's hers." Miss Rose picked up the phone and dialed a number and after a few seconds spoke into the receiver.

"Girl, where you at wit my car? I don't care what you doing. Your brother just got out and you need to come home now." She hung up the phone, looked at Solo and smiled. "I still can't believe you're home."

"I'm here though."

"Yeah, there you are. That was your sister. She should be on her way. So what do you have planned now that you're out?"

"Try to survive."

"I'm serious."

"So am I."

"And that's all you're thinking of doing?"

"Of course I'm a get a job. But I'm thinking of going to school or starting a business."

"What type of business?"

"I don't know. Maybe a barbershop, but I'm really into this music thing."

"It sounds good. But how do you plan on paying for all of this."

"What's that supposed to mean?"

"You know exactly what it means. I was hip to everything you did in your life remember nothing's new under the sun. You might fool the rest of them but not me."

"I ain't about that no more."

"We'll see."

"I've been out not even two hours and you already tearing me down."

"I'm just concerned that's all. Nothing's the same when you're not around."

"Well give me a few weeks to run around a little bit before you start bashing me."

"I'm just being me. I believe that's your sister pulling up now." Miss Rose said when she heard a car engine cut off then a door slam.

Solo noticed that his sister walked straight in and made him realize that the front door was unlocked the whole time. Shaneka, Shay for short, was older than Solo by two years but they could pass off for twins.

After the hugging and kissing, Shaneka grabbed her brother and pulled him toward the door. "Come on, the girls are gonna die when they see you."

"Where you going now?" Miss Rose asked getting tired of Shay using her car like it was hers.

"To go get the girls."

"You better be putting gas in my car wit all this ripping and running you doing."

"I got you grandma."

"Let there be no gas in there and you'll be riding the GTA."

"So what's up, how does it feel to be out?" Shay asked as she maneuvered through traffic.

"Shit, I'm free."

"I know that's right. I got this girl I want you to meet. She remind me of you when we were growing up."

"But she ain't me."

"I know she ain't you. But that's my dog. She a couple years younger than you though. "

"Is she fucking?"

"I don't be in her business like that, but I know she ain't no virgin. Holla at her, if she give you some that's on her."

"Where she at?"

"She probably at home. You want me to call her?"

"Yeah, do that, but I'm telling you Shay, if she ain't real I'ma hurt her feelings."

"Whatever nigga. You might get ya feelings hurt."

"Bitch please, you could never fuck with me and you just like me."

"I'm older than you so you better get it right."

"If you say so."

"I say so."

They went on like this until they got to the daycare where his nieces were. After kissing and hugging them, they got in the backseat and put on their seatbelts. Shay took her time heading back to their grandmother's house, just so she could give herself time away from the hassle of living with Miss Rose.

Shay picked up her cell phone, dialed a number and waiting a few seconds before handing it to Solo. "Here."

"Who's this?"

"That's Keisha, the girl I was talking about."

"Oh, okay," he said before putting the phone to his ear.

"Yo, what up?"

"Who's this?" Keisha asked from the other side.

"Solo."

"Oh, you're sister told me about you."

"Oh yeah, what she tell you?" Solo asked cutting his eyes at Shay. Keisha began giving him a run down of what all she heard. They held a conversation the whole way to Miss Rose's house. Solo handed the phone back to Shay and gave a quick snicker.

"She scared I'm a hurt her yo."

Shay grabbed the phone and mouthed some words in it before hanging up. "I don't know what she scared of, Niggas be getting out the joint putting it down, freaking and all."

"Whatever."

They pulled into Miss Rose's driveway and got out. Solo had already been staying with Miss Rose off and on before he went to prison. Shay came down from Boston with her two kids and took up the other two rooms. When Solo walked into his room he saw that it was left the same way it was five years ago. He knew his grandma only came in here just to vacuum and dust. He opened his closet door and looked at the rack of clothes sitting on their hangers with plastic dry cleaner bags on them. He figured he probably couldn't wear nothing but a shirt or two and his coats. That was because they were already extra big before. He could care less about the clothes. His real reason for going in his closet was to make sure Miss Rose actually didn't snoop around and find something.

The only way to find that out was to find Precious. Precious was the name of his gun, a P two twenty six Sig Sauer German/Swiss with seventeen shots. He closed his bedroom door and went back to the closet. Parting the clothes on the rack, he reached to the back of the wall and pushed. A part of the wall flipped open and he stuck his hand in and felt around until he touched a small box. Pulling the box out he flipped the wall shut and went to sit on his bed. When he opened the box he looked into it and saw Precious staring back at him.

He picked the gun up real slow as the past floated back into his mind. He had went to war so many times with this one gun and came out on top that he needed nothing else. That's why he named it Precious.

Quickly he broke her down and began to clean her. When he was finished he loaded her back up with fresh bullets he kept especially for her. He hoped that he would never have to use her again, but when he put his finger on the trigger, he knew it would be like old times. He also knew that he didn't have much of a choice but to use her again. Because no matter how much he tried to let it go, he could never forget how or why he went to prison in the first place. A war was about to break out real soon and that was one thing he didn't want anyone trying to stop.

CHAPTER 3

Solo woke up around four o'clock in the morning. He still had to shake off those prison hours he was used to. As bad as he wanted to go back to sleep he couldn't. His body was full of adrenaline from being free, but who was up five in the morning on a Wednesday? He sat up in bed and thought for a few minutes. He had to get a job to keep his grandma off his back. He also needed some clothes and some more doe. Damn, he thought. There was too much to do and he didn't know where to start. He knew that this was gonna be his most challenging game. He laid back down and felt a lump under his pillow. He reached under him and put a hand on Precious and knew the answer to his problem. "Sorry ma, but old habits are hard to break," he said to himself as he jumped out of bed and got dressed.

Roger had been at the liquor house all night trying to win his money back. The powder he had snorted earlier had worn off and as bad as he wanted some more, he wasn't about to get up from the table. He started shuffling the three cards in his hand, then slowly peeked at them. He had a full house, Aces over. He looked up into the eyes of Solo who had lost three hundred of his winnings already. Solo had came in at five thirty, late for a liquor house that closed at six. Still, it wasn't unusual, because a lot of drug dealers did that.

Those who were out all night or trying to catch the early shift and wanted a little firewater to get them going. Nah, that wasn't the problem. The problem was that everyone knew Solo and had heard he was in prison for life. Now here he was losing money after which had to be no more than a week out. He was known for getting money, but nothing lasts forever in the penitentiary. Roger knew that, because he had done a few bids himself. He wasn't no slouch either. Plus, he had lost too much money to let anyone intimidate him.

He quickly raised the pot. He watched as everyone else folded their hands. Everyone except Solo. Solo went in his pocket and put his hundred on the table. It was everything he had, but all he did was crack a grin like it was nothing. Roger could feel sweat beads forming on his forehead. He didn't know if it was the coke, liquor or the fact that he was being bluffed. He knew that there were only a few hands that could beat his, but with a full house and aces pulling the odds were in his favor.

"Fuck it," he thought. "I call." He said and turned his hand out.

Solo was a bit nervous when he made the last bet. It was all he had left to his name, if he didn't win this pot he was assed out and definitely at a stand-still. He had won and lost a few hands but this was the biggest pot of them all. He kept thinking how easy it was to win in prison for stamps and hygiene items. This was totally different when over a stack was at stake. He and Roger were the last two standing and both had gone all in on this hand. He tried not to show his nervousness but his bouncing leg was a dead giveaway.

When Solo heard Roger say "Fuck it" he slid his hand to his waste for Precious. He had no intention of losing this hand period. He was going to walk away with this pot one way or another. He saw the three Aces and two fours and sighed with relief. He didn't blame Roger for going all in he would've done the same, but he was glad that it wasn't a winner.

"Rog my man you play some good cards, had me scared as fuck."

"What the fuck you talkin bout nigga either turn out or turn in I ain't got time to keep fucking with you."

"Damn calm the fuck down,". Solo said then place his hand down with the cards stacked on top of each other. There was a king on top and as he slowly slid the top card to the side you could see a queen.

"Man quit with all the suspense," Roger stated feeling like a winner when he saw the two cards that were of different suits.

"I love them queens yo, especially when they stick together," Solo said as he spread the rest of his hand out revealing four of a kind.

"Mother-fucker!" Roger yelled banging his fist on the table. "Man, I need that money back yo," Roger stated feeling like he could knock Solo out take his money and haul ass out of there.

Solo stood up and pulled the money together ignoring Roger's words. Once he had it neatly in a pile he lifted his shirt and placed the money in his pockets. His eyes never left Roger's. He wanted to see his reaction as he got a glimpse of Precious tucked in his wasteband. "You got it youngblood," Roger made known as he lifted his hands up in surrender.

"I know I got it, da fuck you thought you were gonna do? Yo,Corey you should watch the people you let in here not good for business might fuck around and have a body on your hand," he made known.

Corey was the one who owned the liquor house and was an old friend of his pops so he knew that he was safe there regardless of what happened.

"It's cool youngn I'll take care of it," Corey mentioned as he watched Solo ease to the door never taking his eyes off of Roger.

"Yea do that."

Solo walked out the door and made his way home feeling ecstatic as he had some better start up money. When he walked in the house he could hear someone in the kitchen cooking something.

"Solo is that you?" Miss Rose asked coming out of the kitchen wiping her hands.

"Yeah, it's me."

"Where you been at this early in the morning?"

"Just out getting my mind right."

"What's in the bag?" Miss Rose asked not caring, but felt like being nosy.

"Some stuff I bought at John's."

"Like what?"

"Some rubbers," Solo responded digging his hand in the bag.

"Boy, I don't wanna see that mess, but I'm glad you got' em cause remember what I told you."

"Yeah, I remember, why you think I got'em" he said heading to his bedroom.

"You want something to eat? I know you ain't had no real food in a while. I got bacon and eggs."

"Ma, you know I don't eat that swine."

"You and your brother kill me with that no pork mess."

"I don't eat beef no more either."

Miss Rose started shaking her head as she walked back to the kitchen.

"But I'd take some of those eggs as long as they ain't cooked in that pork grease. And some orange juice."

"Some milk?"

"I'm lactose intolerant."

"I knew it was one of you who couldn't take that. I always thought it was Shay."

"Nah, it's me. Tell me when it's ready." Solo said before going in his room and closing the door. He quickly locked it, threw his gun on the bed and dumped the bag of money beside it. He knew that there had to be about two g's there, being that he lost five hundred and he wasn't by himself. There were like three other people who lost just as much. He sat down and began counting.

When he got to fifteen hundred Miss Rose called him letting him know his food was ready. He hurried up and wolfed down his food and went right back to his room. After he finished counting the money, it came to twenty-two hundred. He knew what he was gonna do, but who he was gonna do it with was what he didn't know. A slight thought of Roger crossed his mind. He wasn't a great threat. Solo knew that from past experiences, but time always seemed to change people, even himself.

Still Roger wasn't a major factor, not now anyhow. He had other things to worry about, like getting more money. He grabbed Precious and his jacket and was out again. He was headed to the only place he knew that could provide you with everything he needed to know. John's curb market.

Solo didn't have a problem with hitting the concrete. After five years on lock who would. He just wasn't sure on how people would react when they saw him. He used to run a lot of these blocks, now he felt like a new comer. When he got to the store he didn't see a soul until he walked into the store. Everybody was there surrounding a video game. Some were posted in the aisles making sales. He recognized one of the cats he was cool with before, but it wasn't much love between them, because of past run ins. Still he was good people.

"Yo, Sleepy." Solo hollered out.

Sleepy was too focused on the arcade game to hear anyone calling him. His five nine, yellow frame was hunched over the control boards concentrating on winning. He was real skinny from snorting powder and never eating. Still that only made him hungrier and mean as hell. He got the name Sleepy from the way his eyes sagged.

"Yo, Sleepy, I know you hear me."

"Man, who da fuck calling me?" Sleepy said turning around eyeing everyone in the store. He started to go back to his game when he recognized Solo. "Oh shit. My nigga. When you get out?" Sleepy asked leaving the game and heading towards Solo.

"Yesterday."

"Man, they say you had life man."

"I did, but money talks."

"And bullshit runs a marathon. So what's really good?"

"I'm about to get on that paper chase."

"Oh so you trying to get doe, huh?"

"Yeah, but right now I need to find Pinero. You seen him?"

"Yeah that nigga live down the street on Shaw. Two sixteen to be exact."

"Bet, good luck, I'm a holla atcha later aight?"

"Do that, I might be able to do some things for you."

"Word." Solo threw back at him as he walked out the door and headed to Pinero's house.

Solo walked up the steps of two sixteen Shaw Street and knocked on the door. At first there wasn't any answer, so he knocked harder. He thought no body was home until he heard the door open and Pinero stuck his face out.

"Who da fuck that knocking on my door like that?" Pinero asked looking through half closed eyes. Pinero was a tall dark skin cat, about six four, two hundred twenty pounds and cut. He and Solo had been boys since Solo first moved to NC. They had been through so much together that they were like brothers.

"Nigga open this motherfucking do' nigga. Trying to act all hard." Pinero wiped his eyes, so he could get a better look at who had the nerve to come out their mouth like that. When he recognized Solo, he opened the door wide with a smile on his face. "Ah, shit, my motha fuckin' nigga home. They told me you had goddamn life."

Solo saw the gold fronts in Pinero's mouth, as the sun caught them, then he looked back and punched him in his face knocking him to the floor.

"Yo, what da fuck."

"Yeah, that's for all those years I did without hearing from you. All those times I carried your ass and you wasn't even there when I needed you. I ought a beat the fuck outta you."

"Man, its hard out here man. Plus, I didn't know where you were at."

"Don't give me that. You know where my grandma stay. And I know you be seeing my sister. And you can't be doin' too bad with them shits in yo mouth like you from the bottom or something."

Pinero got off the ground holding his jaw and acted like he was gonna say something when Solo cut him off.

"I don't even wanna talk about it though. Ain't no love lost. That shits dead. What I wanna talk about its getting this money, ya heard?"

"What about it?" Pinero asked still kind of upset from getting punched.

"What about it? You know more than me. All my connects are gone. So I need someone new. Can you handle that?"

"How much you got?"

"I got fifteen."

"Damn, you been stacking ain't you?"

"Don't worry about it."

"Let me call Cool Daddy. He got some Frank."

"Tell that nigga to come correct or don't come at all."

"Man, I got cha." Pinero said picking up the phone and dialing a number. After talking for about five minutes, he hung up and turned back to Solo. "He said he'll give you two onions. That straight?"

"You said its Frank right?"

"Yeah, these fiends be swarming for it."

"Aight, I'll take ya word for it."

"You ain't bullshitting is ya?"

"Come on man. You act like this something new. You know how I get down."

"I'm saying you just got out."

"The world don't stop spinning when you locked up. I gotta get mine while I can. And if you thinking about the feds. They don't make me or break me."

"I feel you my nigga. I just don't wanna see you back in there."

"It ain't like you gonna come see me no way. But what up wit that nigga, Rashawn?"

"Who?"

"That nigga who testified on me, man. You ain't heard nothin'?"
"I believe he'll break west. Plus, he don't get out till next year."

"Oh, I got something for his crab ass."

"I told you I would've got that nigga Dizzy for you."

"Don't worry 'bout it, he didn't know no better. As long as Rashawn don't pop up, I'm straight."

"But yo, I do be seeing Toya and Tonya though."

"Oh yeah, where at?"

"Same place, Southside. Tonya got a little boy by that nigga Saint."

"Yeah, I remember her being pregnant when I was going to trial. I'm glad I never stuck dick to her, end up messing up my bloodline."

"There go that nigga Cool now, pulling up."

"That nigga better not shit me man or he a goner." Solo said pulling out Precious.

"Man, he straight man. This nigga about money. He ain't on that bullshit." Pinero said getting up and heading to the door.

"He better be."

Pinero opened that door and let Cool Daddy in. Cool Daddy was a dark brown cat, an inch or two talker than Solo, with a big head. He use to go to school with Pinero before he got up with Solo. He was doing his thing on the drug tip, and kept a low profile.

Solo didn't like him and it was his first time seeing him. The vibe he gave off was a scary one. Solo always felt that if you were scared of what you do, then don't do it. He thought about robbing him, but he knew it wouldn't be worth it. If he was gonna rob him, it had to be for more than two ounces. He rather follow him home and take everything.

Pinero took them in the back room and they made the transaction. When Cool Daddy left, he locked the door and closed the blinds, then went into the room with Solo.

"You straight?"

"Yo this shit gots ta be some raw. I can smell it through the plastic."

"I told you."

"Yo, go get me a plate, some bags and a razor."

When Pinero got back, Solo sat at a folding table and started cutting one of the ounces up. He put the other one in his coat pocket. When he finished cutting half of one up into dimes and twenties, he pushed the half towards Pinero. "Here give me four fifty."

Pinero looked at him and started smiling. "Nah, I'm straight."

"Man take that shit nigga. I know you motherfucking broke. Trying to front. I know when you ain't got shit."

"Aight bet. You said four fifty right?" Pinero asked swallowing his pride. He always had a hard time keeping money. He was a 'get by' person. That's all he kept, enough to get by.

"This me you talking to. I'm home now brah. I'm a take care of you nigga," Solo said getting up. "Write ya number down. So I can get back with you when I need to re-up."

Pinero grabbed a pen and paper and wrote his number down.

"Yo, you know they hiring at the Waffle House. If you trying to get a job."

"Yeah, I do need that. Which one?"

"On Wendover, by Celebration Station. Come out tomorrow and I'll put a word in for you."

"What time?"

"Between seven and two."

"Seven and two? In the morning?"

"Yeah, I'm telling you its mad broads out there."

"I might come through," Solo said heading to the front door with Pinero on his heels.

"Do that."

"I'll holla," Solo said walking out the door. He knew he needed Pinero more than he showed. It didn't have anything to do with the connect. Pinero was his man. He'd die for him. It didn't seem that way when he got locked up. But on the street whatever Solo asked him to do, there wasn't any questioning or second guessing. He had found a piece he needed. Someone who knew the game and how it was played. Pinero was his right hand man. His bishop.

CHAPTER 4

It had been a week since Solo stepped out of his state browns and into his official colors, green. But for right now he was in black shoes and pants with a Waffle House shirt and visor on, taking orders. Pinero wasn't lying. Chicks came through constantly, but his mind was more focused on getting money than women. Plus, he had to deal with Keisha, who had somehow gotten the number to the cell phone he just copped two days ago and was blowing it up. All that fronting she was doing, now she ready to give a nigga some play.

Solo always felt he had women under control and could get what he wanted out of them. His momma labeled him a lady's man as soon as he could talk. Still, he never thought anyone could break him out of his composure. Not until today. He didn't know if it was being away from real women that made him think what he was seeing was that fly, or the simple fact that that was what she was. When she walked through the door, it seemed like everything stopped. Well to Solo it did.

She was sporting the long weave, with designer shades covering her eyes. The diamond stud in her nose let him know that she was a bit ghetto.

'A ghetto chick wit doe', he thought as he tried to analyze the bumps and curves hidden beneath her Baby Phat sweat suite.

Before any of the other waiters could notice the lady sitting at the counter, he quickly took out his pad and headed her way. "Can I help you?" he asked trying to sound professional.

"Yeah, let me get the cheese steak omelet, has browns, smothered and a large orange juice." She answered in a voice that sounded like she could work as a phone sex operator. She reminded him of Rosie Perez, his all time favorite female.

"Anything else?"

"Nah, that's it."

Solo turned to give the lady's order and knew he had to have her. He didn't know why, but the vibe she gave off was hypnotizing. When he returned with her order, he watched as she pulled her shades off and placed them on top of the counter. He didn't want to stare, but his mouth wouldn't let what he wanted to say come out. He didn't have a problem with talking to females, because he had a gift for it. Still it had been a while. Just when he felt that he found his voice, she looked up from her plate to see Solo still standing there staring at her.

"Don't I know you," she asked squinting at him as if that would help place his face with a name or something.

"Nah, I don't think so."

"I got to know you or seen you somewhere before, for you to be staring at me like that," she said, but not in a nasty or sarcastic way. In fact she was grinning at him in a playful way.

Solo felt she was trying to handle him like he was a nobody. But he was never one to blow his cool. He just glanced at her one more time and started wiping the empty part of the counter. When he finished he stopped in front of her.

"Truthfully, I wasn't even looking at you. I was looking past you," he said pointing out the window at a lady who was putting some bags in her trunk.

"Oh, excuse me then," the girl said after looking in the direction of his finger.

"Don't worry about it. It ain't like you come here unnoticed," Solo said feeling himself again. He knew it wouldn't take much to get back in the rhythm of things. He was just side tracked by this girl's beauty, but he didn't want her to know that.

"Oh, so you were checking me out?" she asked eyeing him knowingly.

"I'm not gonna front, I was looking, But shit, who wouldn't?" he said looking at her seriously. He wanted her to know that he was a real nigga not the play play type.

"But you do look kinda familiar. I just can't put my finger on it. Where you from?"

"I stay on the eastside."

"Nah, not that. Where were you born? I can tell by ya accent you weren't born down here."

"Oh, oh, I'm from Boston."

"Boston. I gotta home girl from Boston."

"Yeah, what part?"

"Manchester, Dor, I'm not sure."

"Was it Dorchester?"

"Yeah, that's it. You might know her. Her name's Angel."

"How long she been down here?"

"For a minute."

He thought for a minute to see if he knew who she was talking about. He knew two Angels, but only one from Boston.

"Is she short, caramel complected, wit da slight slit in her eyes?"

"Yup, I got two cousins down here too."

"Yeah, I know Angel. That's my girl. When the last time you seen her?"

"I believe yesterday."

"The next time you see her, tell her Solo said what's up."

"Solo? The same Solo that stayed next door to Shanice and Terri?"

"Yeah, that's me. Why what's up?"

"I knew I knew you. You don't remember me do you?"

"Uh, uh, am I suppose to?"

"I'm the one who use to come over all the time. Kenya."

"Kenya? You use to wear ya joint in a pony tail right?"

"One of the few dark skin girls wit 'real' long hair."

"Yeah, I remember now, what's been going on wit 'cha?"

"Nothing really. Just handling this business."

"What type of business you in?"

"I'm not really into a business yet. I'm going to school right now."

"Taking what?"

"Business Management."

"You ain't decided what type of business you wanna invest in yet?"

"Nope. And make it so bad I graduate next May."

"It looks like you need to step ya game up."

"I know right. You got any ideas?"

"Music and realty is where the money's at."

"I'll keep that in mind."

"Your food's getting cold."

"I'm alright. I'm not hungry anymore any how." She said going into her purse to pay the bill.

"Don't even worry about it. I got that."

"Thanks. It's good running into someone from back in the day instead of these vultures."

"What's that suppose to mean?"

"You know how niggas be. All up on you thinking you a slut or a hoe, because you wear certain types of clothes. Women been getting raped and what not."

"You might hafta cut a few niggas, let the streets know you ain't even wit da bullshit."

"Yeah, like I'm a go around slicing people."

"Hey, you da one brought up da raping stuff."

"Anyway. Look there's something I always wanted to ask you."

"What's that?"

"All those times I came over Shanice house and you joked around with me. How come you never took it any farther?"

"Ah, man, come on. You were like what thirteen, fourteen? Two years under me..."

"So. I heard about you. How you were running around when you first came to Greensboro."

"So, what's that's suppose to mean?"

"I was just asking."

"Honestly, since you asked. I knew you wanted me to, but I didn't think you were ready."

"And what about now, you still think I'm not ready?

"It's been like twelve, thirteen years now. I don't know what you ready for. What you getting at anyway?, Solo asked knowing what she was getting at, but not understanding the angle she was coming from.

Kenya bit down on her lower lip, like she was in deep thought. "I know Terri told you I had wanted to get up with you back then."

"And you still wanna do that after all these years. I thought you were trying to dodge us vultures?"

"Sometimes past wants are hard to let go. Plus, you aren't one of those vultures I'm talking about."

"And what makes you think that?"

"I don't know. I just do."

"I'm known to break hearts."

"I'm willing to take that chance, plus I'm not fragile."

"You taking a risk because I just got out da joint and I ain't got shit."

"Don't worry 'bout that. Matter of fact," Kenya said pulling open out and writing her number down on a napkin. She didn't believe in anything being coincidental or accidental. Everything happens for a reason. And she knew running into Solo again was meant to be. "Take this number, when you figure out what you wanna do, call me."

Solo watched as Kenya got up to leave and saw how she put an extra switch in her hips. He looked down at the napkin she left with her number on it and knew he'd be calling her. There wasn't a doubt in his mind that he'd call, because he never passed up an invitation.

It was just first he had to find out where she fit in his big game plan, then he'd know how to deal with her. He had to make sure everything was done on his terms, with perfect thinking involved. She could be his queen, a lesser piece or just a plain distraction. Only time would tell, but he knew that once he had his queen, everyone else would fall into place.

Solo snapped out of his train of thought and went back to work. First he took care of Kenya's bill, then waited on another customer. Even though doing his job made him forget about what he was thinking earlier. He knew his head'll be filled with those same thoughts all over again.

CHAPTER 5

Rashawn was the grimiest person you could come across. He cared for no one and didn't live with any morals, creeds or codes. When it came to the streets, there were no rules, anything went. He called it survival. The streets called it snaking. He was an informer for the police. Trading information in order to walk the streets. It never played into his conscious that he was a dead man walking. That at any minute a bullet would end his life. Not only that, but he was pushing it to the max. For a small price he'd set anybody up. That's what he did to Solomon Divine, but it didn't go the way it was planned. He was paid by David Hexal, the leader of a gang named the Congrejoes, to set Solomon up. Not to go to prison but to be killed. Someone else ended up getting hit instead of Solomon. So instead of trying it again, they made it seem like it was him who did it.

The only reason Rashawn became an informer was because during Solomon's trial, they found out he was wanted and facing a habitual felon charge. Deals were made and he got out of twenty seven years with a seven to nine.

The set up had exactly what was needed, two guys and two girls as eye witnesses. The only thing was the other guy, Dizzy. He was wanted too and ended up with five years. Though he didn't do nothing but two of them. See Rashawn and them didn't know that Solomon rolled with the Sangres, a main rival of the Congrejoes. As soon as it hit the prison yard what happened, Dizzy didn't last another day. He was raped and hung from the bars in his room.

Rashawn's only reason for surviving was because of Solo. Once Solo found out what happened to Dizzy, he demanded that Rashawn not to be touched except by him.

A lot of things were unknown on both sides. Solo didn't know why he ended up in prison for a murder he didn't commit. He took it in stride, but wouldn't sit still until he was released. Rashawn didn't know that Solo had won his appeal and was waiting on him. Neither one of them knew that Roberto was behind all of this confusion.

"I'm telling you, that's what he told me, "Rashawn said talking to the Federal agent in a sealed room on the prison unit. He only had a year and a half left before he did his minimum sentence, but he didn't want to do that. Five and a half was enough for him. He wanted to be free. Lately, he could feel and see the tension on the other prisoners' faces.

"And what was that?" the agent asked him.

"That he had a million dollars worth of cocaine under his house and he had his wife and cousin getting rid of it for him."

"Is that so?"

"That's my word."

"You'll write that down?"

"After you put our agreement on paper."

"Not good enough, I need it in black and white."

They went on like this until an agreement was made and they left. Rashawn went back to his cell with a smile on his face, knowing that any day now he'd be free. What he didn't know was that he had just signed his death certificate.

CHAPTER 6

Solo laid on his bed with his eyes closed thinking about life. It never seemed to be what it appeared like. Sometimes you ended up in situations you thought you could avoid. Nothing was the same anymore, but the game had to be played out. He opened his eyes to sight of Keisha. She was sitting astride him with sweat pouring down her face and head cocked back. She looked like she was in pure ecstasy. They had been going at it for the last thirty minutes and Solo was losing interest. It wasn't like before. In fact, he was glad that it wasn't like before, because before was straight booty.

At first, she didn't want to be his first piece after coming straight out of prison. She had heard the stories of how ex-cons be trying to tear a girl's stuff up and she didn't want to experience that. It was funny to Solo, because the majority women want a man who can do it all night and know what they're doing in the bedroom.

His thoughts were right though. After the first time they had sex, it was a done deal. Keisha was open. Solo was mad because the sex was no good. He told Pinero this, but he kept saying "Those rubbers' will mess everything up. That was until he told him that he went in her raw. Now it was known that what she walked around with was no good.

Oh, he still used her to get off, but that was it. Plus, he had someone new he was working on and wanted to spend more time breaking down. Right now, she was in Minnesota as an intern until summer semester started up.

"What's wrong?" Keisha asked, stopping to look down at Solo.

"Do you love me?" he asked her seriously, as one of her sweat beads burst on his stomach.

"You know I do. Why, what's wrong?"

"Didn't I tell you not ta fall in love with me?"

"Yeah, I remember you saying that, but I couldn't help it, you're so sweet and adorable," she said rubbing her hands across his chest as she started to lean down to kiss him. Solo turned his head sideways to avoid her sweaty lips.

"Don't."

"What's the matter, you don't love me anymore?"

"I never loved you. And I told you not to love me, because I'd only break your heart."

The one thing people hated the most about Solo was that you never knew when to take him seriously, because he stayed smiling in the most heated situations. If he was smiling, then his patience has worn thin and he isn't to far from having a spasm. Like now.

"So what now? You saying it's over?"

"That's exactly what I'm saying. So get your clothes and leave."
"You ain't shit," she said getting up and grabbing her clothes off of the floor.

"I already know that. Too bad you didn't find out till now."

Keisha started mumbling some words under her breath, loud enough for Solo to hear as well as set him off.

"Bitch, who the fuck you think you talking to?"

"Who you calling a bitch, nigga? You got me fucked up with one of these other broads or something, cause I ain't the one."

"Bitch, I'll call you what I want, when I want. And if you don't get the fuck out my grandma's house, I'll throw you out. Matter of fact come here," he said reaching over and grabbing her by the back of her neck. He led her to the front door and pushed her out with just her panties and bra on.
"When you see me holla," he said slamming the door.

The day was young and the ringing of his phone meant there was money to be made. He walked butt naked to the bathroom to take a shower, hoping Keisha wouldn't be a problem. He knew he'd be seeing her again, because she was his sister's best friend.

Really he didn't care, but he loved the women of his family and didn't want Shay to be ragging on him. He'd wait to see what would happen and take it from there. Right now he was focused and needed no more distractions.

"I only have three dollars, but I can suck"

"Don't worry 'bout it. Here," Solo said handing the crack head a nickel piece. "I ain't seen you all day. So what I want you to do is go stand by that bridge and catch those cars coming through."

"I don't mess with strangers."

"Don't give me that shit Sarah. Your first trick was a stranger. Do that for me aight? I'm trying to get outta here."

"You gonna look out for me?"

"Don't I always?"

"Let me go hit this and I'll be right back."

"You better hurry up, cause if I'm gone before you make any money. I'm a treat you like a stranger."
"Don't act like that Solo."

"Then hurry up," he told Sarah, knowing she'll try her hardest to get back and pull a few tricks just to get a couple of pieces of Solo's crack. He had some of the best product on the block. With Sheila and Rain being the other competition.

He wasn't worried about them though because police were watching them closely. Rain stayed bouncing from crack house to crack house. It was good, but the customers didn't like him. If they had less than fifteen, he wouldn't serve them. Plus, he was gorilla pimping them trying to make them buy his dope. Sheila's dope was good, but you got less than what Solo gave you.

A lot of people tried to say McConnell road was dead since they closed the projects down. Solo knew different. It was flooded with money. The majority came from the prostitutes who walked the strip. They all loved Solo, because he was about his business and turned no one away. Some of them tried to come on to him, but he let them know that he didn't trick. None of them wanted to trick with him, they just wanted to fuck him. So he fucked a few and got some head from others. The only one he didn't mess with like that was Sarah. He considered her special. Not in the way that you'd consider your girl, but as a good friend.

He remembers how she came to him on his third night on the block. In the matter of an hour she had dropped by every twenty minutes to spend nothing less than fifty. She had heard that he had some diesel and decided to pay him a visit. Ever since then, she's been a dedicated customer.
The difference between her and the other female crack heads or crack heads period was that she didn't have to have any money to get some dope.

He'd give her some yay off of G.P. and ask for nothing back. The only reason was because she made him so much money she deserved it. Because of her, he was supplying two boarding houses, a section of Ray Warren projects and half of McConnell.

Not to mention the people she turned him onto that lived in different spots. Yeah she was a gold mine in her own right.

Solo was sitting on the porch of his boy Hue, that's whose house Sarah had went in to smoke her dope. It wasn't a crack house, because he didn't run it, but a lot of the fiends came.

Here to get high. Most of the time Solo sat on Hue's porch just to talk to him, but he also served everyone that ever stepped through his door.

"I see you got them hoes in check," Hue said. Hue was an old school cat from DC. He got high too, but as a professional carpenter he could afford it. Even though he was a smoker, Solo respected what he said, because it was coming from a man with experience. There were plenty of days he would come around just to kill time and talk to Hue. His neighbor was on some other shit. He didn't want Solo serving around him, but he'd let the fiends smoke in his house so he could fuck them. Hue wasn't any different. Because as old as he was, he was still trying to slide in something.

"Man, I don't be stunting these broads. They ain't got nothing for me, man."

"You can't tell them that. All you hear is Solo this, Solo that. Where Solo at? When he getting here? That shit be having me mad as fuck. They know you come through everyday around the same time."

"That just be that fire they wanting."

"Nah, these bitches don't even be smoking half of what they be buying. They think they can go straight and get cha."

"Man, get the fuck outta here man. You need to take a break. Matter fact give me my shit back man," Solo said jokingly reaching for the shake bag he had given him.

"I'm dead ass man. You got these bitches going crazy. I ain't never seen a fiend want a nigga more then they want a piece of crack and I've been on this same strip since it was a dirt road."

"Old school, peep game. You of all people should know this. Those bitches don't want me. It might seem that way. They just wanna get close to that stash and rob a nigga blind. And I ain't having that. Plus, I got a girl for now."

"You might be right, but I'm telling you, they after your ass."

"Man you a silly nigga."

"There go Beverly, now watch what she do."
Beverly was one of the better looking fiends on McConnell that pulled in a lot of tricks. As soon as she turned the corner she spotted Solo and came up on the porch.

"Hey Hue. What's up Solo?"

"What's up?" he answered back as Beverly sat in his lap and wiggled around a little bit.

"You straight?"

"Yeah, what you need?" he answered and could feel her hand snake between his leg before he finished his sentence.

"And I ain't doing no deals," he said putting her in her place before she got carried away.
I ain't come over here for no deals. I came over here to cop. You act like I ain't got no money."

"Then why's ya hand on my dick?"

"I don't see you moving it, so you must like it there."

"It don't make no difference to me. I'm too focused on this money to let little sex games interfere."

"Bitch cop and blow. You making my spot hot wit all that small talk," Hue barked at her, sounding mean, but telling the truth.

"Fuck you Hue. Give me twenty," Beverly said going in her shirt to get the money.
After they made the transaction, she got up to leave and made it a thing to squeeze his Johnson before doing so. Solo being the man that he was grabbed her ass in return.

"Hmmm. Whenever you ready to get some of this holla at me, "she threw at him.

"I don't trick."

"Who said you'd be tricking? It'll be all on me," she said walking off with a switch in her hips.

"See, that's what I'm talking about. You heard her for yourself. And she ain't never walk like that since I've known her. All of'em like that. I'm telling you they after you," Hue stated seriously. He knew Solo seen it, but he just had to let it be known openly.

Solo could hear his phone ringing from inside Hue's house where it was recharging. He went to go get it and when he answered it he could hear music playing in the background.

"Yo."

"Solo, you gotta get over here."

"Who dis?"

"P man."

"What I gotta be over there for, I got money to make."

"You can pump that over here. There's some people I want you to meet."

"Like who, cause I ain't up to meeting nobody right now."

"These niggas Sangre but I'm not sure about this one cat."

"I left you in charge nigga, now you don't know who repping our shit?"

"That's what's wrong wit ya'll niggas. Ya'll let any and everybody get down. Then it fucks you in the end. Don't let nobody go nowhere. I'm on my way," Solo said before hanging up.

"Yo, I'll holla at 'cha later Hue."

"What you got team trouble?"

"Something like that. If something big come through call me and see if one of these moterfuckers got a big screen for sale," he threw back as he started walking up the street. Pinero's house was only five blocks away and every step he took was done with pure anger. He was past mad, because he had worked hard for his position. Putting in more work after work. Making sure things ran smooth and in order. If Cassidy got whiff of him letting snakes into the garden it was over.

Yeah, he had to see what was going on and fast.

When Solo stepped into Pinero's living room all he saw was green. Green hats, sweat bands, shirts and bandanas. He thought about what he was seeing and how it related to the grass that carpeted the African nations. This is what he truly lived and died for, seeing his people come together. He didn't care whether it was in the street or in a university as long as they untied.

Pinero quickly let it be known who Solo was, then he pointed out the guy he wasn't too sure about. Solo studied him a bit, but couldn't put his face anywhere. He only recognized three of the people there. Kase, Chaos and Diamond. Kase and Chaos were like twins. They did everything together and had gotten down on the same day. Solo had put them down after hearing about them all over Greensboro as some live wires. He didn't like messing with a bunch of trouble makers, but he felt that under his guidance he could utilize their energy and make them a deadly force. They were what he called his "Black movers."

They went out and set shops up wherever there was money to be made. He had no doubt in his mind that they would be happy to jump start the train again. Standing at six two with two hundred and thirty pounds of solid muscle a piece, Solo knew they were unstoppable. Their dark complexion and shoulder length dreds completed the package of intimidation. What Solo's mental eye saw were two rooks. He cut his eyes at Diamond, a bronze colored girl that came from her own Columbian and black heritage. She was the definition of a true female gangster.

At five-five and petite, you would think she was a brush off, but that was everybody's mistake. She was a third degree black belt in Tae kwon do, as well as a golden glove, ranking number three in her weight class. He met her outside of the club one night shooting it to some guy's the ass. He went to break it up because he was riding dirty and didn't need the police snooping around.

"Chill Shorty, that's enough, that nigga don't want no more."

"He better not. And anybody else who disrespect me can get it too."

"Aight, You done?"

"Yeah, I'm done," Diamond said stopping to catch her breath.

"What's ya name?"

"Diamond."

"Diamond, I like that. I'm Solo. You here by yourself?"

"I was wit that nigga."

"I'll tell you what, since you done made the spot hot, I gots ta go. But I see something in you, so I want you to call me and we'll talk," Solo said writing his number down and handling it to her.

"What makes you think I wanna call you?"

"You took the number didn't you?" he said walking towards his car.

"Solo," Diamond called after him before he got into his car. She saw him stop and felt a little nervous. "I ain't trying to take up your time, but could you give me a ride home?"
Solo looked at her and smiled. "Sure, get in."

From that moment on they formed a bond. He never once sexed her or ever tried. That made her respect him more. She became the first female Sangre to get put down under him. After she put in so much work, he put her in charge of recruiting all females. It felt good seeing all the familiar faces. But there was someone missing, his boy Cross.

"I see you got all my people together, but where's Cross?"

"Cross is down in Florida handling some business," Diamond spoke up. He left Cross under her care because he was the youngest one he had on his team. And Solo knew she'd take care of him like a mother.

"What kinda business?"

"Your kinda business."

Yo, everybody get out except for ya'll four," Solo said pointing at Diamond, Kase, Chaos, Pinero and the off brand guy.

"What's ya name yo?"

"Drake."

"Drake, huh? Who came and got you Drake?"

"Bobby."

Solo automatically knew he was lying because Bobby was still diggin' and hadn't earned enough stripes to bring anybody with him. He looked at Drake and seen why Pinero phoned him.

Drake looked like he would fit in better with the Congrejoes than Sangre.

"Aight Drake, I just wanted to know who you be, cause I never seen or heard of you before. But I'm a talk to Bobby and see what's up witcha. You aight? You need anything?"

"Na, I'm straight."

"Good, go outside wit the rest and let me talk to my people."

When Drake walked out the door, he turned back to the four left in the living room.

"Bobby ain't bring that nigga," Pinero pointed out.

"I know he lying. Kase, Chaos, I want you to watch that cat. If anything seems funny get in touch wit P and we'll deal with it."

"Who you think he is?" Diamond asked.

"I think he stands by for the Congrejoes, but I don't wanna jump the gun, so we'll watch him and see what's popping. It's good to see ya'll again. I've noticed ya'll've built a strong nation.

But I hope nann one of you went and got a fake nigga. Cause you know the consequences. Everyone who comes wit ya, carries your name and is your responsibility. If you don't know I've only been home a month and I ain't playing any games this go round. P what's da status on our run?"

"It never really stopped from before. Everybody's done stepped back in their position so we back to where we were. We got blocks on the South, North and East."

"What about the west side. That's where them crackers and big spenders be at."

"Those people will be scared to death to see one of us in their hood."

"I'll tell you what. Whenever Cross come back put him on it. He'll know what to do. And Diamond, I need you to get one of your girls with a clean record to get me an apartment and a car. Ya'll been out here driving for the last five years, while the Police been driving around in my shit."

"You think so?" Chaos asked.

"Man, I just seen my shit while I was walking over here."

"Baby don't worry I got 'cha," Diamond said.

Solo looked at her and could sense the secret desire she had for him.

"Good look, D. Yo, I'm out yo. I'll holla back later. Hit me when you hear something. Everyone of ya'll aight." Solo watched them all in agreement.

"Yo, Kase, Chaos don't forget what I said. Watch that nigga. Drake." Then he was gone.

CHAPTER 7

Solo woke up to the smell of something exotic and some soft music that sounded like a waterfall. He reached between his legs and felt the stiffness that came from his dream. He was thinking of Kenya, but thoughts of Diamond kept interfering. He felt as if he was losing his mind, because he never looked at Diamond any other way but as family.

After using the bathroom, he walked into the living room and saw Miss Rose on a pile of pillows meditating. Not wanting to disturb her, he tip-toed to the kitchen and got some eggs, turkey bacon, turkey sausages, Eggo waffles and some orange juice.

Just as he was putting the eggs in a pan and waffles in the toaster, he saw Miss Rose appear in the kitchen doorway.

"Hey Ma, what going on?"

"Doing a little soul cleansing. I hope your gonna eat all that," She said pointing at all the food he had cooking

"Of course, I'mma eat all this."

"You eat like you only eat once a day or something."

"Sometimes I do."

"I need you to do me a favor."

"And what does that happen to be my dearest grandmother?" he asked, knowing that anytime she asked him to do something it was going to be some serious labor.

"Clean the kennels in the back. Feed and bathe them wolves too."

"All of 'em?" he asked thinking of the nine full-blooded wolves that she bred in her backyard.

"Yea, baby. I'm getting too old to do all that now and I got some people coming over to look at a few of them.

"Now I know where I got my game from."

"Thank you sweety."

"I guess I can do it, since I be eating your food all up, huh?"

"Now you're catching on."

After doing everything Miss Rose wanted him to do and helping her sell three pups, he had a little bit over an hour before he had to go to work.

"Solo, phone," he heard his grandma hollering as he stepped out of the shower. He went in his room and picked up the phone.

"Yo."

"What's da dill Pickle?" a soft rugged voice asked.

"Who dis?"

"Ya brother!"

"What up fam? Why it take you so long to call?" he asked not really caring, because him and his brother weren't as tight as they should've been.

"I only call every once in awhile to see about them people."

"You still on the wanted list for child support."

"Yeah mon."

"How much you owe now?"

"Those motherfuckers got me owing them five g's."

"Damn, brah. You only got one seed right?"

"Yeah, but I ain't paid them in five years."

"I can't promise you nothing, but if I can, I'll shoot you a few dollars maybe get them niggas off ya back for a while."

"Nah, I'm straight."

"If you say so. Don't say I ain't ask."

"Where you at now?"

"ATL."

"Word, that's like the Garden of Eve."

"You mean Eden."

"Nah, Eve, where all the women be at."

"Yeah, but they ain't ready for this Bostonian nigga. You oughta come down and chill for a bit."

"I might just do that, but I gotta get my shit together first."

"Yo, whenever you ready just let me know. Grandma got the number. I'll send you a plane ticket or something."

"You got it like that?"

"Not yet, but it's in da makings."

"What the music thing?"

"Yeah. You, you still play chess?"

"Of course. And I'm ready for ya ass too."

"No you not, but I'll play you whenever."

"I gotcha. But yo, I gotta go to work. So I'll holla at ya another time."

"Do that."

"One."

"One."

Solo hung up the phone and thought about his brother. Shakim was the oldest now since Tyrone died. Growing up, Solo and Shakim use to fight all of the time. They would go at it until Solo went and got a knife, then all the brotherly tussling would stop. At times Shakim felt guilty about being mean to his baby brother. He tried to make it up by doing little things like taking him to the mall, park or zoo. He was always back and forth between their mother and father's house, so there was no way to really bond. Age brought about a better understanding between them and they became a little closer through the chessboard.

Now Shakim was in Atlanta trying to get things popping off and Solo had to go to work.

"Ma, you know I'm moving in a few weeks."

"You never said anything about moving. You only been out a month or two."

"Three to be exact. I just need some space."

"Where you going?"

"I'm moving off of Julian."

"You a grown man so I can't say nothing. I just hope you know what you doing."

"Trust me grandma, I know I'll be okay. And I won't be home tonight."

"Why not?"

"I'm supposed to be staying at this girl's house."

"You and them women. You better be sure, cause once I lock that door I ain't opening it back up."

"I'm sure."

"Okay then, go on and get outta here before you be late."

Miss Rose always thought of Solo as her little baby that would never grow up. Because he always had a way with women, she never let it bother her what she knew he was doing since he was twelve. She picked up a picture of her daughter Linda, Solo's mother. She was holding a week old Solomon Divine and thought of her other two kids. Holly and Jackie. Linda was the youngest and her most dearest. Thinking of her being gone brought tears to her eyes. She never thought she'd be burying one of her own. That's why she treated Solo like the son she never had, to take the place of his mother. And she knew no matter what that she'd always be there for Solo.

CHAPTER 8

Except for the weekend, there wasn't a day Solo wasn't on the strip. He had put in so many hours that he felt like he was working a full-time job and the Waffle House was something on the side instead of vice versa. It won't be long before he quits though. He had another job offer with more pay and better hours. $9 an hour for five hours of work, he couldn't beat that. Plus, the fact that he'd work from one to seven with an hour break, he'd be able to juggle his hustling time however he wished.

It's funny how times change, some for the good, some for the bad. Money makes the World go round was one of the truest statements ever made. But money also gives birth to greed, because you never feel that you have enough. Just like a kid in a candy store, their eyes are bigger than their stomach. Solo tried not to fall into this category. He knew everything had its limit. All he wanted to do was get in and get out. But while he was in he wanted to gain as much as possible, so he could accomplish what he had planned for him and his people.

"Ay, yo, Hue man. You ever wish you could start over?"

"What you mean youngster?"

"You know, like given a new fresh beginning, without all this bullshit in ya life?'

"Let me pull ya coat ta something, but you gotta think. If we were given the opportunity to go back and do things all over again, we wouldn't be able to, because we wouldn't be aware of what will happen, so we'd do it anyway."

"But what if we could go back knowing what we know now?"

"It wouldn't matter, because whatever you change will change something else and the results will still be the same. God has our lives already planned out for whichever path we take. It's your choice to be apart of one or the other. The outcome only he knows, but there is one already made for you."

"Like chess."

"Yeah, like chess."

Solo looked at Hue for a few seconds and wondered. He wondered what Hue would be doing if coke or heroin never touched the black community. He probably would've never met him, but they wouldn't be doing what they were doing either.

"I didn't know you could get so deep like that."

"There's a lotta things you don't know about me Youngblood. That's what's wrong wit you kids nowadays wanna know everything, but won't take the time to learn nothing. But I can give you this much credit, you're different, cause you listen. At times I wish I had a son to talk to and tell him the things I be telling you. The American Dream has no room for the black man. We can have everything them crackers got, money, big car, big house, beautiful family, even own our own business, but we still get looked down on. There's no hope."

"So you just gave up? You ain't never try to make a change?"

"Look at me. I'm a motha fuckin' drug addict. What can I do? Plus, the people got ta want to change in order to make a difference. I can't do it by myself. I can easily start it, but who'll keep it going once the torch gets too heavy in my hand? That's what I want to know Solo, Who?"

"Me. I'll keep it going."

"You can't do it. Ya not a man yet. Ya not ready for responsibility."

"I can do it."

"Nah, ya too stuck in da streets. Ya intentions might be good, but da way you achieve them is bad."

"How can you say that, I treat you good don't I?"

"Do you? If you really cared you'd stop feeding me and everyone else this poison and get us some help. Cause as long as you give it we gone take it. I'm too far gone to say no."

"I never knew you felt like that."

"All of us feel like that. Don't nobody wanna be a junkie, but some of us are too scared to admit it. Like I said, I can't do it on my own. It's gonna take someone like yourself to change it all around."

Solo was clinging to every word coming out of Hue's mouth and knew what he was saying was, if he cared he'd stop what he was doing, but he had things that needed to be done now, and there was no faster way to get money than this. He wanted to tell Hue something, anything to ease his mind, but there was nothing he could say. His phone rung interrupting his worrying.

"Yo".

"I got them government twins for ya," he heard Cross say over the phone. Cross had come back in town last week and quickly jumped on locking the Westside down. Cross was only 20, but mature for his age. Solo had brought him along because he like molding people and the last 4 years you spent in school was the best time to learn. Cross reminded Solo of himself when he was younger. Wild but determined. He wasn't wild like crazy wild, it was just his ideas that were wild. Whatever he wanted to accomplish, he'd do it with no problem. They use to call him the "Negotiator", because that's what he did.

He had that school boy look that no one could turn down. But those who did were making one of the biggest mistakes in their life. He wasn't by far a slouch. That's how he became Cross. It had nothing to do with the 3 crosses he wore around his neck, one for the mind, one for the body and one for the soul. It was because he loved crucifying people.

"Where at?" Solo didn't miss one beat with who Cross was talking about.

"The Oasis."

Solo knew he what he was talking about an area they had outside of the city limits, but he had forgotten about it. It use to be a stash house, until the Feds got whiff of it. He figured since it had been 5 years and Cross was out there, then everything was kosher. He had put in too much work with Cross for him to let him down, but if it ever came to it He'd kill Cross before he let him betray him.

"Yo, Hue, if I ain't back by 8, I'll holla tomorrow aight?" solo said getting up.

"Aight young blood. You gonna leave me somethin'?"

"Nah, your rehab starts today."

Hue watched Solo get into his new forest green Denali that Diamond had got one of her troopers to cop. He didn't want anything big and fancy that would attract attention, but Diamond wanted to spoil him.

Solo pulled out of the drive way and stopped up the street to pick up Double Deuce and Barry. They were true crack heads and knew they'd do anything for a hit, let alone the 8 ball he was willing to give them if they did what he wanted.

When they pulled up to the Oasis, Solo only saw one vehicle, an old Ford pickup with a bed cover. He knew it belong to a crack head because nobody in this crew wanted to be caught in a piece of junk. They got out and Solo went up to the house and knocked.

"Who dere?" he heard Cross' deep southern dialect come through the door.

"It be that Notorious nigga."

"About time," Cross said opening the door.

"What up?" Solo asked wanted to see what he had.

"Who dat?"

"They extra help. Ya'll go sit on the couch over there till I call you."

Cross took him into the back room where he had Toya and Tonya tied up and blindfolded. Pinero was sitting in a chair facing both of them.

"Take their blindfolds off." He told Pinero

"How ya'll lovely ladies doing?"

Both Toya and Tonya recognized Solo at once and started blabbering their mouths

"Shh, shh, it's alright. I understand. The police were pressuring you, you were helping your boyfriend and brother. Yeah, I know all this. But it isn't what I know, it's what you didn't know. You didn't know who you were fucking wit. I'm da reason you breathin this long. And to think you thought you'd never see me again cause they gave me life. I want you to remember. Money talks and bullshit runs a marathon. Strip 'em and tie them backwards to the chair." He told Cross and Pinero.

He watched them diligently as they did what he said. When they were finished, Toya and Tonya looked liked they were ready for some backdoor action. He called Deuce and Barry in the room and gave them some uncut crack mixed with xtacy pills that he had made up especially for this.

"Have fun fellas, smoke that first and if they give any resistance, don't be scared to persuade 'em anyway you like," Solo said as he walked out the room and closed the door. He could hear the 'government twins' screaming out and begging for mercy. He wondered if they knew that the next nearest house was 2 miles away. He didn't really care if they did or not. He knew they'd be in there all night and he didn't feel like waiting till they were done.

"Whenever they done drop them bitches back where you found 'em. Deuce and Barry can be let off anywhere on the eastside. I'm out.

"You sure you wanna keep 'em alive?" Cross asked not sure of what to really do when they were finished, cause he didn't want to drop them back off, but if Solo said so, it was out of his hands.

"They're a better warning for da rest of them bitches who wanna be a snake wit their man," he told him with such seriousness, that you could see it in his eyes. That's how much he hated snitches.

"If you say so."

"I say so." He threw back walking out of the house.

CHAPTER 9

Solo wasn't the type who liked crowds, so going to the club was the last thing on his mind. But his boy Pinero kept pressuring him into it. After a while he broke down and went to the club. It was lady's night at the 'Screaming Parrot' and they had gotten there early. A little too early. There was a rule you went by. 'Never enter the club before 12. It didn't matter what the cover charge was, you always let the women catch that before 12. Solo knew why that unwritten rule was made. There wasn't a soul around, except for about 10 or 12 people and it didn't matter that the Triads number 1 radio station was there. To kill time Solo drank a few Ice Houses, then a glass of Paul Masson.

He never had a problem with holding his liquor as long as he had something on his stomach. The liquor didn't take effect until he had a Thai Ice Tea. He looked for Pinero, who had been running back and forth to the bathroom when he looked up and saw Kenya making her way to his table. He sat up just as she bent down to give him a hug. He could feel all eyes on him. That's when he noticed how packed it had gotten. He looked at his watch and seen it was 12:30 and wondered where the time had went.

"Why haven't you called me?" Kenya asked wanting to truly know.

The average man never turned her down, but she had to realize that Solo wasn't an average man. She didn't know what her real attraction was to him. It wasn't like he was unattractive, that he was far from. She had plenty of attractive men, but she like to have the best and most wanted. That's what it was, to be able to obtain what others couldn't. So she stood in front of Solo waiting on his response, not knowing that he was a bit tipsy.

"You said when I figure out what I wanna do to call you. Not a second before."

"So you saying after 3 months you haven't given me one thought?"

"Oh, don't get me wrong, I've thought about you, but I haven't come to a conclusion."

"Is there anything I can do to convince you, I'm the one you need?" she asked placing her hand on his knees and getting face to face. She made it so that he could see down her dress top at her 34Ds, but he didn't bite.

"Slow down Jezebel, it ain't that serious. Matter fact come wit me," he said leading her into a dark corner of the club.

He didn't need to get up to say what he had to say, but in order to be in control of the liquor he drank, he had to start moving. "I see you done shed a few clothes for us vultures and rappers."

"Don't even go there."

"Let me explain something to ya. This shit right here," he said running his hands down her dress. "Doesn't impress me. It's what you got up here," he gestured at his temple. "I can care less about a broad who looks good but has nothing on her mind. I'll take a tomboy with a brain before I'll take a Jet Beauty of the Week who doesn't know shit. You feel where I'm coming from?"

Kenya was in her own world with Solo being the other person there. When he started talking he had got up real close to here, because of the noise around them. He never knew that she had zoned out on every word that he spoke into her ear. So it took her awhile to realize that he was waiting on an answer to what he said. She opened her eyes and even in the darkness, could see the seriousness in his eyes and knew that she couldn't play around with this man. "I knew I couldn't come to you half ass, but I'm probably as real as they come. I'm book and street smart. Plus, I have a lot to offer."

"Like what?" Solo asked showing some interest. He was becoming intrigued and wondered why he really held out on her. Instinct is what held him back, but he didn't want her to think she was getting anywhere with him. Not yet, anyhow.

"If I told you, then you turned me down, what good would it do me?"

"Then what good is it doing me?"

"When the time's right or if there's a time you'll know." Solo looked down at her and realized how short she was compared to him. He only stood 5" 7", so she had to be no more than 5' 1". He knew when he was being challenged and he couldn't front like he didn't like it. Nor could he front like he never thought of Kenya. In between doing a 5-year stretch, he thought about every girl he encountered intimately in North Carolina. There were a few and Kenya had popped up once or twice in the ranks, but he never could remember her name. You had to use your imagination a lot, especially since they stopped letting sex magazines come through the mail. He had passed up a lot of opportunities in life, there was no good reason to pass up anymore. Plus, Kenya seemed determined and ready to dedicate herself to the cause.

"I'll tell you what. We both grown, so let's stop playing games and get up outta here."

"That's what I've been talking' about. Let's go."

"Yo, I came wit my man, so let me tell him I'm bouncing, I'm rolling wit you right?"

"Yeah, if you want to."

"Aight, I'll be back."

Kenya watched Solo disappear through the crowd and had to catch her breath. She didn't know what was wrong with her. This was what she wanted, but Solo had caught her off guard.

She looked at her watch. It was 1:30. What were they gonna do at 1:30 in the morning. It was obvious, but she wasn't thinking straight. She needed to get a hold of herself, so she quickly went to the bar and ordered a blue motorcycle. Just as she was letting the last bit of liquid roll down here throat, Solo popped up.

"Ok, I'm ready."

Kenya gave a start and a bit of liquor rolled down the side of her lip. Solo caught it with his finger and licked it. "You aight?"

"Yeah, let's go." She said smoothing out her dress and heading for the doors. When they got outside she headed straight for a new Silver Diamante and stopped. "You hungry?"

"A little bit, but ain't nothing open this early."

"Don't worry I got it," she said getting in the car. They pulled off and headed up the street to the 24 hr Wal-Mart.

"Where we going?"

"I just need to get a few things right quick," she said getting out and going inside.

Solo didn't feel like waiting, so he got out and followed her. He watched as she went to the grocery section and dripped some chicken breast, fettuccini and a bag of iceberg salad into a carry basket. He quietly stepped off to the entertainment section and thought about how big Wal-Mart had gotten.

From a regular discount store to adding a grocery store that could compete with Food Lion and Winn-Dixie. Plus, it was open 24 hours. Whoever owned the company had a good marketing division. These were the type of people he needed to invest in, instead of the streets. This was where the money was, amongst the frugal consumers.

"There something you want?" Kenya asked from behind.

Solo didn't like being snuck up on, a lot of people end up in the hospital that way, but he didn't show his surprise.

"I was just looking at a couple of movies I hadn't seen."

"Get 'em"

"You sure?"

"Yeah."

He picked up two of the videotapes and handed them to Kenya.

"Ghostdog and Love & Basketball, aight let's go."

When they got to the register Kenya pulled out a credit card and Solo wondered if she really had doe or was she like every other black person who thought that a card meant free money never mind the credit. When he was younger his father had a habit of putting things in his name. He still believed that his name was probably on every bill in his house.

It took Roger a lot of liquor and weed to build up the courage to do what he was about to do. Everyone tried to talk him out of it, but he couldn't let being robbed go. He had been waiting to catch Solo off guard and his patience was finally gonna pay off. He saw when he had left with some girl and went to follow them, but just as he was out the door a fight broke out and he got swept into the crowd. Again, he thought he was gonna break loose but it was too late.

Solo was gone and all he saw was the car's backlights shining in the distance. All of a sudden shots rang out and people began running. Out of the 3 shots that were heard, 1 hit air, the other was lodged in an Avalanche door, the last ended up in the back of Roger's head.

"I wondered what happened down there?" Kenya asked when they saw the ambulance fly pass them.

"I don't know, but I hope nothing happened to my man" Solo said pulling out his phone and dialing Pinero's number.

"Yo, I'm just checking to make sure you aight."

"Some nigga just got popped son."

"Word, who?"

"I believe Roger from the Dust bowl. A stray hit him."

"Word, but yo, I gotta go, that ain't my concern. I was just checking on you."

"Aight then I'll holla."

"Aight be safe." Solo said hanging up.

"What happened?"

"Somebody got shot."

"Who?"

"It ain't my concern."

"Damn you cold hearted."

"I ain't cold hearted, I just don't give a fuck, cause if they would've shot my fam, I ain't got time to care about who I'm a kill."

They rode in silence for a while, but Kenya couldn't take the way Solo stared at her.

"Why you keep looking at me like that?" she asked cutting her eyes at him every so often, so she wouldn't lose focus of the road.

"Like what?"

"Like you're not sure about something."

"Maybe I'm not, but I could be wrong, it depends on how you act."

"Sometimes you make me wonder myself."

"Then curiosity is killing both of us."

"Yeah, curiosity, if that's what you wanna call it."

They talked a little longer before pulling in front of her apartment. He noticed that she stayed out near the airport and wondered how much it cost. All of those thoughts quickly disappeared when Kenya got out of the car and headed up the stairs. He watched as her ass moved back and forth in a dress that looked more like an extra long tee shirt. Her flawless calves reminded him of when he and Pinero used to have a calf fetish. Now it was an ass fetish, probably the reason he couldn't keep his eyes off of the one in front of him. He quickly grabbed the Wal-Mart bag, got out locked the door, and followed Kenya inside.

When they got inside he put the groceries on the counter and took a seat in her dining room. The liquor had found its way out of his body and he felt that he needed a drink.

"You got something to drink?"

Look in the fridge, there ought to be something in there."

"I think I need something stronger than some fruit punch."

"Well look through the bar in the living room."

He walked in the living room and saw the bar immediately. She had every type of alcoholic beverage that a regular bar would have.

"You gotcha own little ABC store jumping off don't ya?" he said looking at the wide selection. He wondered if she'd like his personal concoction, he'd have to try and find out.

"You never know what special occasion might pop off."

"I know that's right," he said coming back into the dining room. "I got something I want you to try."

"You ain't trying to poison me are you?" she said jokingly.

"Come on, if I wanted you dead, best believe I'd be no where around the murder scene."

"What is it?"

"Something I made up called Bloodbathe," he said handing her a glass.

She took a sip and waited for a while to get a feel of what she was tasting. "It's good. Smooth, but strong. What's in it?"

"Can't tell you. You might try to sell my recipe."

"Boy please. If I wanted it that bad, I'd take it."

"You could have it as long as you could take the ass whooping with it.'

Kenya ignored that last comment not knowing if she was to take him serious or not. She continued cooking the food she had bought. After they finished eating they went upstairs to watch one of the movies.

Upstairs Solo layed at the head of the bed with his head propped up on her pillows. He was looking like Al Bundy, with his pants unbuttoned and hand stuck in his boxers. Kenya had changed into a pajama top that came down to the top of her knees and he could easily see that she was naked underneath. She was laying opposite of him, so when he cut his eyes to the right, he could see straight up her nightgown. He had gotten to the point where he felt that he had waited long enough to make his move.

Still he wanting her to think it was her making the first move. The movie was so boring that he had to catch himself from nodding off. He thought since the RZA had something to do with it, that it'd be hot. How wrong he was. And it didn't take long before he found something else to garner his attention. He reached over and started tickling Kenya's feet.

"Boy, quit it," she said laughing.

He did it again.

"Quit it."

He did it one more time and she reversed her position, lying in the same direction as him. He had been forgot about the movie, so he started focusing on other things. For the next five seconds he stared at her taking in the prettiness of her face. He looked at the way her eyes slanted a bit, her ears, eyebrows, even the way her lips were parted. He could've done this for the rest of the night if she didn't turn to look at him.

"What?" she asked.

"Nothing," he answered, but kept staring at her.

When she looked up again she didn't say nothing. She just kept looking from his eyes to his lips. Solo leaned over and covered her mouth with his own. As she slid her tongue out he could taste the Italian dressing that they had earlier on it. He reached up and grabbed her right breast with his left hand, then slid it down her stomach to the inside of her thighs.

Feeling the hot wetness, he flicked a finger over her clit and heard her moan beneath him. She quickly pushed him back and got up. At the same time Solo slid his finger under his nose and came back with a smell similar to jasmine. He watched as she pulled her nightgown over her head and dropped it on the floor. He peeled out of his clothes and just threw them, not caring where they landed.
"Cut on the light," he told her.

"For what?" she asked, cause she was used to having sex with them off.

"Cause I want us to see each other," he answered picking up the remote to cut the movie off and put the slow jams station on.

When Kenya cut the light on and turned back around she could see what he meant. Looking at him laying there naked, she could see all the muscles in his chest, arms and abs poking out. She could also see the cuts he suffered through from his prison wars and the bullet wounds from his street wars. Still none of that mattered when her eyes took in the length of his manhood and wondered if she could handle it. She felt that she had no choice, if she was to make him hers.

Solo didn't move while Kenya looked him up and down. He watched her face go from wonder and concern to complete surprise, when she looked between his legs. He was used to this. A lot of girls shied away from him because they weren't used to taking lengths as long as him.

That's why he wanted Kenya to turn on the lights, so she could see what she was going up against. Also, so she could see his war marks. The only scars he had that weren't from going to war were three lines across the left side of his chest that stood for Love, Respect and Territory. The main principles of the Sangres. Kenya saw and knew this but said nothing of it. Some things were better left alone.

As Solo's eyes wandered down Kenya's body, he took in the flawless of her skin, with its toffee colored complexion, due to her Black and Asian parents. He looked at her firm apple sized breast, the flatness of her stomach and couldn't see her having had any kids. When he glanced at the thickness of her thighs and trimmed pubic hairs, a spot on her lower right side next to her belly ring caught his eyes.

It was a tattoo of a woman with a fork in her hand leaning over a plate of money with the initials M.H.C. under it. He thought that it looked familiar, but couldn't quite grasp where he had seen it before, so he let it go and finished looking her over.

"Are you finished?" Kenya asked impatiently.

"Yeah, I'm finished."

"Well, what do you think?"

"Perfect," a little bit too perfect he thought. He had a true belief that no female was 100% perfect, that they all had some type of flaw. He couldn't find anything physically wrong, but he knew something had to be or it would put a dent in his theory.

Kenya crawled on the bed, like a sneaky alley cat, until she was face to face with Solo. "You ready?"

"As ever."

She softly kissed his lips and he closed his eyes as she went from head to thighs, covering him with wet kisses. When she kissed his eyelids he laughed, but when she stuck a pierced tongue in his ear he shuddered. She traced the three lines on his chest and pecked at all of his knife and bullet wounds. As she passed over his stomach, she looked up at him and paused.

Going to her nightstand, she pulled out a feather tipped tongue ring and switched it with the one she had in her mouth. Back between his legs, she grabbed a hold of him and flicked her tongue out teasing his family jewels. She felt his leg jerk when she took one sac, then the other into her mouth. Pausing, she looked at his erection and wondered if she could deep throat it.

Solo put his hand on the top of Kenya's head, urging her to continue. When he saw her head bobbing up and down and the way her lips stretched over him, he layed back and closed his eyes. After about ten minutes went by, she stopped and straddled his waist with his joint standing up like a flagpole behind her.

"You got some rubbers?" he asked her not too sure about going raw.

"Am I gonna be your girl?" she asked back while leaning over him. She looked into his eyes as they started changing colors, which only happened when his mood changed.

He thought about her question and figured it wouldn't hurt to see what type of woman she would be by his side.

"Yeah, I believe I can do that."

"Then you don't need a rubber," she said and before he could object she slid down on him, letting a 'Oh God' pass between her lips when she got to the hilt of him.

Solo let out a soft chuckle at her response to him being all the way inside her, but this was only the beginning. He looked at how her breast bounced around and the slight grin on her face and knew that she felt like she was in heaven.

He didn't want her thinking that she could handle him, so he grabbed her by the waist and flipped her, over, not once pulling out of her. He hovered over her for a few seconds letting her catch her breath.

"Now are you ready?"

Kenya was still enjoying the sensation of being fully stimulated and felt if it got better then that she was more than ready. She whispered yes and nodded her head at the same time just in case he didn't hear her.

Solo had a thing with letting women experience the pains and pleasures of having sex with him. That's how he had turned most of them out. So when he eased into her it was only half way. He listened to every moan she made with each stroke as if it was a new song he was trying to memorize. Just as she was getting use to the rhythm, he switched speeds and rammed into her hard and fast.

He treated her like she was his enemy and was using himself like a knife to torture her. Her cries of anguish mixed with the 'oh gods' and 'oh shits', did nothing but urge him on. When he did stop, he pulled out with a squishy pop that sounded like a shoe being pulled out of some mud.

Solo felt the sweat build up all over his body. He always told Pinero that he didn't need to lift any more weights because he worked out in the bedroom. And right now he was about to do another exercise. "Turn over," he told Kenya raising up on his knees.

Kenya layed there for a second looking at Solo's manhood still fully erect and glistening with her juices. She wondered if anyone ever died from having sex. She heard of men having heart attacks, but she wasn't thinking of that. She was thinking of a woman getting fucked to death, cause that's what it felt like Solo was trying to do, kill her. Still this is what she wanted and what she asked for. She could blame no one but herself, because he did warn her. She gave out a sigh, eased up and rolled over thinking about what that girl said on that Timberland song "Love 2 Love ya." 'Big girls don't cry, they take all of it."/doggy style, like George and da Parliament."

As Solo eased into her, he knew that Kenya hadn't experienced anything close to what he was putting her through. He didn't really care, but he did like knowing that he left a big impression wherever he happened to go. When he looked down he saw Kenya had eyes squished up, biting the sheets and gripping the pillow like she wanted to tear it apart.
He knew she had something so he gave her the chance. "Whose pussy is this?" he asked while ramming into her as hard as he could.

"Yours" a low gasp came out.

"Who you say?"

"Yours motherfucker, yours."

"That's what I thought and you better not give it to no one else," he said grabbing her by the shoulders, so she couldn't bury her face and started driving into her harder than ever.

"Ohh, fuck me. Motherfucker, fuck meee." Kenya screamed out sounding like a possessed demon. Now she knew what the pain and pleasure of having sex with a real gangsta was like. This was Eve's "Gangsta Loving." All those other so-called thugs weren't even capable of doing half of what Solo could. She was on the verge of climaxing and didn't want her orgasm's built up to stop. She didn't care what she was saying or that spit was forming at the corner of her mouth. All she was concerned with was getting off.

Solo was about to bust, but he didn't know where to put it. He thought about letting loose on her back, but he didn't want her complaining if it shot in her weave. Nor did he want to disrespect by shooting all over her linen. By the time he decided where he was gonna put it, it was too late. He ended up unloading a stream so long and thick that Kenya's walls couldn't hold it all in.

Rolling over weak and exhausted, he instantly fell asleep, not caring if she came or not, but knew that she did somewhere along their fiesta. Nor did he hear her telling him that he was the best, which he had heard plenty of times before. He had just put in two long hours of work and was tired, but deep in his dream state, he knew that Kenya would be the one beside him when everything came together. He let his hand hover over this queen, but never got to fully grip her before total unconsciousness took over.

CHAPTER 10

Two months later and everything was running smooth. He had made a few phone calls up north to his own people, who only went out their way when serious money was involved. Now he had big shipments coming through, but he needed more, except he didn't have a company that he could send it through. He'd worry about that later, he had to focus on the here and now. And what he wanted to do was a major rule in this type of hustle. At first the money was topsy-turvy, because his people were grinding hard on every side of town, but he wasn't greedy. He let other dealers get theirs too, but they had to pay a block tax. On top of that he put word out that here was some new crack out called Kamikaze, because it was damn near suicidal to take. In actuality it wasn't any different then what he already had out there, except it had less cut and a smear of acid in it. Word spread fast and a new breed of fiends were born.

Solo never was the show and tell type of person, so he let Pinero play the front man while he ran everything from behind the scene. He thought back to the conversation he had with Hue and knew he was far from getting out of the game. He wanted to ease out of it unnoticed, but that was in the future.

There were a lot of moves to be made, more pieces to be sacrificed. This game was just beginning, to end it now would defeat its all around purpose.

Sitting at home in his easy chair, feet propped up and watching TV, he held on to a glass of orange juice and Grey Goose, while a hollowed out cigar packet with half a ounce of weed burnt in an ashtray. At 9 o'clock in the morning, this became his breakfast. It wasn't like he didn't have any food. It was just that he wasn't use to taking care of himself. If Kenya or Diamond didn't come over and cook, he never went out the way to. Some would say he was lazy, like Miss Rose did whenever she popped up and started cleaning up behind him. Others didn't bother to say a thing, cause his only reply would be 'I'm a grown ass man.'

He started noticing his drinking level go up and his grandma warned him about that. Telling him how that fire water don't sit well with Indians. That's how they took the land from us. Got us drunk, then killed and raped our people. Then wanna say it's a Thanksgiving. Yeah, those were her exact words. It wasn't a habit, not yet anyway. This wasn't his everyday routine, far from it. The only thing he did make sure he did every morning was watch the news, but today felt different. His conscience was running crazy with guilt, tearing at his brain. Too much money was being made, meaning stomachs were empty somewhere. A lot of kids were at home hungry because of their parents' addiction and he was one of the reasons they were addicted.

One of his rules was to give back to those who suffered the most from his dealings. Meaning, since the kids were suffering that's who he had to give back to. Christmas was a little over three months away, but he figured he could do something early.

Plus, he didn't celebrate the holiday anyway. He called Porsha, who worked at the bank where he kept his money. She also happened to be Kenya's best friend.

Good morning, Nation's Bank, how may I help you?" a soft voice said over the line.

"Yes, may I speak with Porsha please? Tell her it's her husband," he asked not liking to have to talk all high class to get what he wanted even though he had done it before for illegal gains.

"Hold on for a minute, sir."

"Yeah, who this?" Porsha asked with an attitude as soon as she was connected to the line, not liking anyone playing games with her. Porsha was a red-boned girl that favored Lisa Raye and had the same type of personality she had when she played Diamond in the 'The Player's Club.'

"Calm ya ass down girl. This Solo."

"Don't be doing that shit. You know these bitches waiting for something to gossip about."

"I'm sorry, don't be mad at me," Solo said putting on his sad voice.

"Whatever nigga. What you need?"

"What's my bank account like?"

"You got a bank book don't you?"

"I don't mess wit that shit, too much paper work. I just make da money." He said lying through his teeth. He kept up with every red cent. He usually had Diamond make the deposits, but he always doubled behind her. Not because he didn't trust her, he knew she was the most loyal out of all his people. He didn't trust the bank.

"I have to go look it up."

"Ain't you near a computer?"

"Yeah."

"Then look that shit up."

"Nigga you better watch ya mouth."

"I love you too."

"Fuck you. Hold on."

And that's what he did. It took her about fifteen minutes before she came back on line, catching him in the middle of pissing.

"I know you ain't pissing while I'm on the phone?"

"I had to piss, yo, what's up?"

"You got about a quarter mill in there."

"Aight, I'm a take about 10 thou out, can you have that ready for me?"

"10 thou, what you about to do?"

"Some charity work."

"Oh, Mr. Hardcore has a soft side."

"Yeah, cause broads like you can't handle it when it get's hard."

"Nigga, please."

"What'll Kenya think if she found out you were begging for it?"

"Fuck you, Solo."

"I would, but you might tell Kenya. Yo, let me stop. I'm gone. Make sure you have that ready for me, aight?"

"Yeah, I'll do that, bye," Porsha said laughing a bit. Solo was a silly guy, but good-hearted. She wondered what Kenya was trying to do, because she saw a lot of trouble breaking out in the near future. As much as she liked Solo, she knew if Kenya pulled one of her stunts on him, she'd have to ride with her girl, even if it cost her her life.

When Solo hung up the phone he sat back and thought for a minute. He still had the charity feeling fresh in his mind, but he didn't know where to start. It was going to be a beautiful Saturday and he didn't want to waste it. School was about to start back up, so he had to make it a time to remember. All he could think of doing was throw a block party. He quickly grabbed his cell phone, cut off the TV and headed out the door.

When the dump truck backed up onto the grass in the field, no one knew what was going on. But as soon as the kids saw all the toys being dumped out, they quickly reacted. They raced to the field not caring who got knocked over or ran over, as long as they got one of the toys. Solo got the idea from Trick Daddy's 'Thug Holiday' video. They treated him the same way, when he stepped in Toys-R-Us until they saw the stocks of money. Once all the toys were claimed, he pulled the food out. Everyone came. Old, young it didn't matter. Free food in the projects was passed up by no one.

After a while people were seen shooting ball, dancing and having a good time. It reminded him of growing up in Boston, where they'd barricade the street and hold a block party. He even went and contacted some local DJs. Up and coming rappers and singers. He convinced them that this was an opportunity for free promotion. He didn't think they would show up on such short notice, but it must've been the word "free" that brought them down.

Of course he had to pay the DJ, but it didn't bother him, because the people were having a good time.

The music was blasting from two huge speakers that sat on the edge of the court not occupied and people were walking around with drinks, of all kind, in their hands.

Solo thought it was funny that every time there was anything resembling a party, women came out half dressed trying to catch someone's eye. He saw women and girls alike, with low riding jeans that showed the things underneath. Halter tops, sports bras, spandex, anything that'll attract a man's attention. The sad part was that it always seemed to work no matter how nasty or stank they looked. The only reason he paid it no mind was because he didn't do much chasing since he got with Kenya. She didn't have him under control, far from it. It was just it made no sense to turn in a Bentley to test drive a Honda.

He watched as people got on stage and grabbed the mic to show off their talents. He vibed when someone harmonized a good song and laughed when heard people spitting trashy rhymes. He felt good inside and he knew that this good feeling was what it was about. Giving back no matter how much or little you received. Just as he was sinking into this feeling, his bliss was interrupted by a pair of hands over his eyes.

"Guess who?" came a feminine voice that sounded like a whisper, even though it was trying to shout over the noise.

"I don't play no guessing games." Solo said grabbing the hands holding his face hostage. When he turned around and looked down, he stared into the face of a girl so beautiful, that he almost forgot who she was. "What you doing here?" Solo asked his niece, Jade.

"My mama brought me"

"Where she at?"

"Over there getting something to eat."

"You get any toys?"

"No."

"Don't worry I'll buy you some later. Go tell ya mother ta come here," he said, then watched as she took off to get Shay.

Shay came weaving through the crowd with a plate in one hand and the hand of her youngest daughter in the other.
"What up nigga?"

"What up? What Quana, you can't speak?"

"Hi, Uncle Solo."

"Come here," he said picking Quana up. He favored Quana over her sister, because they shared the same birthday and almost acted the same. "What you been up to?"

"Nothing."

"You been good?"

"Yeah."

"You ain't get no toys neither huh?"

"Nope."

"Don't worry, your Uncle gonna take care of ya."

"You do all this ya self?" Shay asked.

"Yeah, why?"

"I'm just asking, damn, don't have a baby. You know police around too?"

"And."

"I just thought I let you know. Cause I see a lot of green flags swarming around."

"Them my people. They allowed to have fun too. Plus, they probably wanna make sure nothing happen to me."

"That's what I mean, cause there's some Congrejoes here too," Shay said pointing at a few people.

"I'm on point sis. Don't worry 'bout me." He said putting Quana down.

"I'm just making sure. You're my baby brother and I ain't trying to lose you like we lost Ty."

"Shay, I was having a good day, please don't fuck it up for me with old memories."

"Okay, you right. I'm saying you could put some burgers and franks out though."

Solo chuckled at her comment. "I was told that I shouldn't took to someone else, what I wouldn't take for myself."

"Bullshit."

"Hey. Why you complaining about what you ain't pay for anyway?"

"You know how I do," she said walking off.

Solo looked at her go and thought about how much he loved her. No one never knew everything about him except her and Pinero. But way before Pinero, Shay was his only confidant. She knew about the Congrejoes and the reason Solo had a personal beef with them. She use to date a few of them until Solo told her not to and why. She respected his wishes because blood was thicker than water and she didn't want to become a risk to her own flesh and blood. She was just as street as he was, but when you had two kids to raise, a sacrifice had to be made. But if it ever came down to it, Solo knew that his sister would strap up if he needed him to.

Rashawn was standing at a distance, mingling amongst the project residents. No one recognized him as the guy who testified on Solo. Five years ago most of these people weren't around, not where most of the were Sangres then. He himself didn't even know that Solo was out here.

In actuality, after five years he had forgot what Solo looked like or who Solomon Divine was. But he did recognize the colors of the Sangres and Congrejoes flashing here and there, but he didn't let it stop him from having fun. He even stopped what he was doing to listen to the guy getting on stage.

Solo got on the stage and stopped the music, so he could grasp everyone's attention.

"Can I have everyone's attention, please," he said waving his arm back and forth. "First, I would like to thank all of you for coming. I hope you enjoyed yourselves. What I'm trying to do is get our community together so we can have more things for the kids to do. Since school is starting, I hope to get some after school programs started in not at the center, at least in the neighborhood, but I'll need all of your support. This is just the beginning of my giving back to ya'll. Understand that the Sangres provided all of this today. Yeah you heard right, the Sangres. I don't want you to be totally influenced in your judgment of us by what you hear. My people have a lot to offer that is very positive if only you'll accept our generosity. Give me time and my actions will speak louder than my words. Thank you," he said stepping off the stage.

"That was beautiful, if I say so myself."

A voice said from behind him and he just told his sister that he was on point. He was losing it, getting too comfortable, like he was immune to bullets. He turned around and looked in the face of Splash, David's second in command. Solo quickly reached for Precious.

"No, I ain't come here for that. I see you have your people out here."

"And you got yours."

"Oh, them. They're nobody, just babies to this."

"What do you want?" Solo asked not trusting Splash one bit. He had survived almost as many wars as Solo. He got the name Splash, because that's how the blood came out of your body when he slit you throat.

"I just had to make sure it was you. All this running around people were doing, saying how Solo was home, it was making David upset."

"Tell David, he ain't gotta worry 'bout me as long as he doesn't disrespect."

"Oh, so you done softened up huh? I don't believe it one bit. You wanna see David, don't you?"

"I never said I didn't."

"So why you talking 'bout don't worry 'bout you? We know what ya beef is and I'd want him dead too. But the lines already been crossed."

"What's that suppose to mean?"

"Oh, you didn't know? You ever wonder how you ended up in prison?"

Solo pulled out Precious and pointed it at Splash and was about to pull the trigger when a voice stopped him.

"Baby, don't do it," Kenya said running up beside him.

"Move Kenya, you ain't got nothin' to do with this."

"Too many people are out here. Plus, the police are patrolling."

"Sweet Kenya, it's so nice to see you," Splash said grinning.

"You know this nigga," he asked glancing at her but not taking his eyes off of Splash.

"Yeah, I know him."

"I see ya'll have some talking to do. I'll see ya around Solo. Take care Kenya," Splash said disappearing into the crowd.

Solo put Precious up, then turned to Kenya with fire in his eyes.

"How do the fuck you know that nigga?"

"Solo calm down."

"What do fuck you mean calm down. I'm about to put a hole in this motherfucka and you telling me not to. What you fucking this nigga or something?"

"He's my brother."

"Your brother? Get da fuck outta here. Since when?"

"Since forever. We got different fathers."

"And you weren't gonna tell me that your brother was the leader of the Congrejoes right had man?"

"I don't be getting into all that. Plus, why would I need to tell you that?"

"Don't worry about it."

"What you mean don't worry about it?" She started to ask, then noticed the green flag hanging out of his back pocket and knew the answer to her question. Solo saw her eyes glance at his flag and started to say something, when one of his people whispered something in his ear. "We'll talk later aight?" he said walking off.

Kenya watched him go, feeling dumb. She knew that Solo trusted nobody and that bother kept a lot from each other, but things were getting out of hand. She never expected things to turn out like this. Yeah, they had a lot to talk about and soon, because sooner or later something was gonna jump off and she wanted no parts of it.

In every crew there was someone who had to stay on point at all times, because one slip up could bring down the entire fort. Amongst the Sangres that was Diamond. She had devoted herself to Solo and made sure he had an extra pair of eyes at all times.

He never knew how dedicated she was, because she always played the background. Something he had taught her to do even while he was in prison. She held him down without him knowing. Every time she wanted to send some money or some type of card, she went through his grandma, who kept it a secret. In fact she was the reason he was out right now.

When his lawyer was ready to give up on his case because his money had ran out, she cleaned out half her account to pay him to continue to work on his case and no one else's. Of course she didn't like him with other women, but she had to respect his choices. At first she didn't care, but that was before she fell in love with him. She was patient, because she knew that it wouldn't be long before they were together. Until then she would make sure she had his back and that meant even now. As she watched the confrontation from a distance, the gun pointing, then Kenya coming into the picture. She knew something wasn't right with that girl and it wasn't that she was with Solo. It was a sneakiness she had about her. She knew now that she had to watch her as well.

Diamond wasn't the only one who had been watching what was going on. Rashawn quickly recognized Splash as the man who paid him for David, but it was the other guy, the one who was up on the stage, who he couldn't place.

He remembered him saying something about Sangres, that's when it dawned on him who he was. But it was impossible because he was there when they gave him life. Still, he wasn't taking any chances. He had to get out of there before someone recognized him. He was trying his hardest to avoid everything green, but he had consumed too much liquor and weed and ended up running from the grass and bushes as well.

As soon as he cleared the projects and started feeling like he got away safely, total darkness overcame him as he was hit over the head and tossed in a van heading to the Basement. The 'Basement' was an abandoned building that use to be an underground car shop slash chop shop. Solo usually held parties here for his people only, other than that he used it for a torture chamber. Anyone that wasn't Sangres or a party wasn't being held, and they were brought down here, never came out alive.

Solo took his time getting to the Basement. He wanted to make sure that he held his composure when handling this type of situation. Even though he already knew what he was going to do, he still wanted to be in total control. When he entered the building he looked around and saw about ten Sangres standing in a circle. He thought that it was a few too many, but then again they needed to know what could end up happening to them if they ever betrayed him. When they saw him coming they parted like the Red Sea and he saw Rashawn tied to a chair. He seemed to be unconscious and that was one thing Solo didn't want. He wanted him to be aware of everything that was about to happen to him.

"Wake him up" he told one of his boys and he saw Rashawn open his eyes in utter confusion.

"Over here, baby boy. You ain't never thought you'd see me again, huh?" Solo asked slowly feeling the rage building up in him as he thought about those precious years of his wasted because of who was sitting in from of him. Still he kept his cool, showing no sign of emotion.

As soon as Rashawn's eyes adjusted to the light in his face, he recognized Solo standing in front of him. "Yo, it wasn't me. I swear ta God it wasn't my idea. They paid me to do it."

Solo came forward and got face to face with Rashawn.

"Who did?"

"That nigga you were talking to in the projects."

"What nigga?"

"The one you got into it wit behind the stage."

"Splash?"

"Yeah, him and David."

"I don't believe him. Raise him up." He told Kase and Chaos, who grabbed Rashawn and tied him to a hook that was used to lift up engines.

"I'm telling you it was David Hexal," Rashawn said as he was lifted in the air.

"Diamond go get my tools," he said then turned back to Rashawn. "David, huh? The same David that leads the Congrejoes?"

"Yeah that's him."

Diamond came back and handed Solo a mini saw, the type used to cut steel chains, then stepped toward Rashawn and stripped his shirt off.

"And he paid you to pin a murder on me?"

"Nah, he paid me to have you killed."

"Oh, really, y'all hear this. I was supposed to die, instead I ended up with a murder charge," he said cutting the saw on.

"And how much he pay you?"

"$50,000."

"50g's huh? I hope I was worth it, you fuck ass nigga," he said placing the saw to Rashawn's chest and making a line down to his nave. The sounds of agony made most of the witnesses scrunch their face up. But the top five sat and watched with disgust on their face. Not the type of disgust you see when someone is about to be sick. It was the disgust shown when you saw someone break the codes you live and die by.

If asked, there wouldn't be a second hesitation to take Solo's place. And the ones of mercy only made them madder. Solo had carved so many lines on him that pieces of skin started peeling off in small chunks slapping the concrete in front of him. Rashawn had to have fainted at least fifteen times, but was revived before Solo continued. After about an hour he stopped and Pinero dashed him with a bucket of rubbing alcohol.

He looked at Diamond who quickly went over to Rashawn and pulled out a Pearl handled butterfly knife. Pulling down his pants she cut his dick off and shuffled it up his ass. A symbol saying to 'go fuck yourself.' She then stood on a chair and gave him a Columbian necktie courtesy of her father. This would've been enough for anyone, but Solo didn't think so. Pouring a gallon of gasoline over the body he summoned to Cross, who tossed the cigarette dangling in his mouth at the already dead corpse.

None of the other Sangres caught onto what Solo had done. He had the closest ones to him participate in this murder. As the body burned, they all did think one thing from what they heard. A war was about to break out with the Congrejoes real soon and everybody's loyalty was about to be tested.

Solo turned to leave and caught a glimpse of Drake in the crowd. "Yo, yo Drake. Come here," he said then turned to Kase and Chaos. "I want you to get with Kase and Chaos and handle that Splash for me, you think you can do that?" Drake looked at Solo with a nervous twitch, not knowing how to respond, but being put on the spot in front of the top Sangres he had to answer.

"Yeah, I can do it."

"Aight, that's sealed. Just let me know when it's done." He said cutting an eye at Kase then nodding his head. He turned and left not saying another word. He didn't have to, too much was already going through his head as it was. It was almost time to begin the game and his queen was already in jeopardy. A lot had to be thought out and fast before everything fell apart.

CHAPTER 11

Solo didn't know why he came to Kenya's house instead of his own. Not before changing clothes anyway. Letting himself in with the key she had given him, he stripped off everything he had on, shoes included, and put them in a garbage bag. Tip toeing through the house he stepped in the bathroom to take a shower.

After he was finished, he walked naked into the bedroom with Precious gripped in his hand. He put her on the dresser and got in bed. He didn't bother to wake her up, nor did he want to. He wanted time to think, but also wanted a warm body beside him. He looked over at Kenya and wondered how she could sleep so hard or she probably wasn't sleep at all. She probably was thinking how mad he was earlier and didn't want to bother him. She knew who was laying beside her, so he ignored her and went into one of his thinking zones. He pulled up the mental picture of his board and sorted out his pieces. Kase and Chaos stood firm at the rook position. Cross and Diamond were his knights. Pinero was his bishop. Kenya and Porsha took up the last important spaces, but they were faint in comparison to everyone else.

He began to analyze his situation. Because of her brother he couldn't treat her the same. He knew that if it came down to it, who she'd pick first, because he knows who he'd pick. Porsha and Kenya was like him and Pinero, so what one knew the other did too. They had to be replaced because a war, his war, was about to break out and he needed every position filled. It was like the military, without the lead commanders, everyone else was at a loss. He didn't know who he could get to step up and hold it down beside him. He was brought out of his trance by Kenya, who had rolled over and threw an arm across his chest.

"Hey baby, when you come in?" she asked in a voice full of sleep.

"About twenty minutes ago."

"You could've woke me up. You okay?"

"Yeah, I was just doing a little thinking."

"About what? What happened earlier?"

"That and some more."

"Is there anything I can help you with?" she asked wanting to straighten things out, so there wouldn't be any tension between them.

"I don't know yet," he answered knowing there was a lot that she could help with.

"Do you wanna talk about it?"

"What's up wit yo brother?"

"Splash lives his life and I live mine why?"

"How close are ya'll?"

"He's my brother, Solo, what kind of question is that?"

"Because that nigga can use you to get to me and if I have to put a hole in his ass I don't want you stopping me like you did before," he said turning his face towards her.

"Why don't you talk to him? Maybe ya'll can squash whatever beef ya'll have."

"Da beef ain't wit him. It's wit his boy David, and since he run wit David he apart of it too."

"And you feel by messing wit me your opening up to your enemy?"

"Exactly."

"So what you wanna do, break off what we got because of that nigga?"

"If that's what you want."

"I don't want none of this shit. Solo look at me," she said pulling his face to her. "I love you."

"Nah, you don't love me," Solo said pulling his face out of her grip.

"How can you say that? Huh? How can you actually lay there and say that?"

"Cause you knew."

"I didn't know shit. Not about you and them Sangres or David and the Congrejoes. Splash is my brother, my family and I can't change that. Just like I can't change what I have of yours."

Solo sat up in the bed letting the covers fall revealing both him and Kenya's nakedness.

"What's that suppose to mean?"

"I'm pregnant."

"Since when?" he asked looking at her stomach and seeing a slight bulge. He wondered how he had overlooked such a thing. It made him realize how busy a person he was.

"Since two months ago."

"Why haven't you told me?" he asked already knowing the answer.

"You've been so busy running around 'on the grind' as you say."

"Still, I don't think it'll change anything though." He said lying back down.

"Why are ya'll beefing anyway?"

"You really wanna know?"

"Was it over some type of turf?"

"Nah, this shit goes way deeper than a petty ass block."

"Then tell me."

"Very few people know this, I believe David told ya brother, but besides my sister, Diamond and my nigga P, no one else knows. This is a serious matter not no play play shit, so if you not ready for what I'm 'bout to tell ya, let me know."

Kenya looked at emotional waves crossing Solo's pupil and knew not to take this as some type of joke. She wanted to know this side of him and was prepared for it. "I'm ready."

Solo cut his eyes from Kenya's gaze and stared at the ceiling.

"In order for you to truly understand, I have to start from the very beginning," he said cutting his eyes at her and when she nodded her head, he looked back at the ceiling and began his story.

"When I was younger...."

Solo, whenever telling this story would travel back, speaking as every picture from each scene would unfold in his mind.

"...Growing up in the streets of Boston was just like everywhere else; you had to know how to survive. The difference between up there and down here is the size, as well as the people you had to go up against. See you might have a few clicks runnin round here, but up there you gotta worry about whole sections. You had Chinatown, Jamaica Plain, Dominicans over here, and Puerto Ricans over there. Whites, blacks, everybody had their own area. Then you had the Italian Mafia and the Irish Mob two of the strongest forces up there. Of course the Irish ran shit, that's why you have the Boston Celtics, but I never liked either one of them. They looked at everybody else like we were only good for hard labor and sex. By the time I was ten, my grandma had moved down here and my mother would send me to her every summer thinking it would keep me outta trouble. But I was a hardheaded little nigga. I was too obsessed wit da streets ta go any other route.

When I was twelve, my cousin Toy fronted me my first pack. This was when my oldest brother Tyrone was alive. He was nine years older than me and I looked up to him like an idol. Damn near worshipped him like one. I followed him everywhere trying to copy his moves. He was like the smoothest hustler out there. He taught me everything. How ta spot undercovers, cut my yay up so I'd get more out of my pack and what kind of investments I should make. This was around da same time that da Irish Mob started taking back over.

By wiping out da Mafia, they done alotta people a favor. They wanted a hand in all companies getting money, except the drug trade. When that happened, people started flooding the block.

Tyrone didn't care no how, cause he was copping straight off da boat and supplying all da second-class dealers. Like I told you I looked up to my brother and wanted to be just like him. So when I found out that he was a Sangre, I ran out and got down. I use ta have this nigga who rolled wit me named Dionante'. He was the only real friend I had. We was like Bill Cosby and Sidney Portier on "Let's do it again." I tried to get him to get down wit me, but he said he wasn't feeling that.

Than one night standing on the corner of Blue Hill and Bellevue just coming from a house party. We were smoking and drinking, you know just kicking it, while I made a few sales. A man came by dressed like a bum and bumped into my brother, then asked for some change. He always told me that if you never gave back, you'd end up losing everything. So I payed it no mind when he went in his pocket and pulled out a twenty. I did see him about ta hand it to him, saying 'here you go.' The dude was like 'thanks and here you go.' That's when I heard the gunshots and my brother was knocked into me, bleeding from three holes in his chest. I wanted to holla for help but, I couldn't find my voice and I started to panic. By da time I got myself together and called da ambulance it was too late. My brother was dead. He died in my arms. I don't know why the guy let me live, maybe out of some type of guilt. But I saw what he looked like and made sure I never forgot either. I tortured myself thinking of that night every time I woke up and whenever I went to sleep. That face burned itself in the back of my lids. The face of my best friend, Diavante'."

"You didn't tell da police?" Kenya interrupted.

"Baby girl, I'm from da streets and we don't do da police thing. Plus, what could they have done. The murder rate is so high up there and I haven't seen a case solved yet. So, no, there wasn't no going to da police.

Anyway, after that happened, mom dukes packed all of us up and moved down here. She said something about getting away from da violence and not wanting to lose any more of her kids to da streets. My pops wasn't too far behind, but it didn't help that he came down because he was da reason all of us were someway or another attached to da streets. Nothing, well almost nothing came good from his side of da family. I still made trips back and forth to visit family and I thought I'd never catch up to Diavante', but I was a determined little nigga. Plus, I had underestimated my family's clout. I knew we had built a small empire of our own. It was nothing compared to da Mob, but we had earned our respect from da streets and legit business owners. But da pain of losing someone that close to me had me fucked up. I couldn't focus, you know? See everybody on my pop's side of da family is straight con artists. Whether it's a scam, soliciting, boosting, hustling, it doesn't matter, male or female, one of us is doing it and there's not a single doubt that we love each other. So when one of us got crossed all us were bein' crossed. They called us da "Darin' Divines" cause we dared anyone ta fuck wit us Yeah, we were ill, in fact we still are."

"Wasn't ya'll Sangres, why ain't they handle it?"

"Let me tell ya. I waited ta after da funeral, grabbed me three niggas and went to that nigga house. I was ready ta kill whoever answered the door. Mother, brother, sister, I didn't care. I was fourteen and ready for revenge. But I wasn't ready ta kill no elder. I was always taught, at home and in da street, never harm a child or hurt da old and that's who so happed ta answer da door. His grandmother. She knew how close her grandson and me were, even greeted me wit a hug and kiss. She said that she hadn't seen Diavante' in about two, three months. When I walked away, I walked away from everything."

"And that's it? What's that have to do wit David and Splash?"

"Listen and I'll tell ya. And don't cut me off no more yo," he said already feeling the anger building up as he told the story remembering everything that happened.

"Okay, I'm sorry," Kenya responded not knowing what to take of Solo's statement. Nor wanting to find out, seeing the seriousness in his face escalate as he told his story.

"I got an uncle named Trace, who back in his day was a pimp in every word. He had all types of exotic women. Filipino, Indonesians, Persians, anyone not from America that's who he fucked wit. They use ta call him Foreign Xchange Trace. He said it was like traveling around da world without leavin home," Solo let out a small chuckle as he thought about the stories his uncle use to tell him.

"He's retired now though. But even at fifty-five he's still bustin'em down. Now he only put that fast talk on what he call "challengeable women." And I ain't talking about them broads who be playin hard ta get, prissy, or stuck-up. Nah, none of dem. I'm talkin bout Chief of Police wives, senator daughters, them type of broads. Just so happen he was bangin da sister of Jimmy Bayne. Jimmy Bayne is like da head honcho over all Congrejo sets on the east coast. They gotta go to him, if they got a problem between sets, wanna open a new set up, whatever, so he keep traffic seven days a week for at least twelve hours out of the day.

One Sunday night after having a family dinner his sister overheard Jimmy and one of his superiors talking. This guy was telling Jimmy about a brave heart that had gotten his "feet wet." That's like saying he's a made man or has shown his loyalty by killin' someone. That brave heart was Diavante' getting down wit da Congrejoes after I asked him ta roll wit me. That nigga knew Ty had rank and controlled a lot of the drug flow. And he knew that getting rid of him would bring them a lot of the street money that was going to da Sangres. So he spit in my face twice. The lady didn't know that da guy Diavante' killed was Trace's nephew, because she didn't know his name. She was just making pillow talk like any other time they were together.

By this time, Diavante' had bounced outta town without a trace.

"Years passed, I got older and earned my own superior rank. I'm da one that flooded da 'Boro wit Sangres, but you would've never figured that out had you not seen my flag earlier. That's because I don't broadcast who I am. I coordinate my clothes ta accommodate my colors.

So if you ain't a real G you'd never notice. Anyway, my family got tired of waitin and was ready ta take out every Congrejoes runnin' through South Boston. That meant Dorchester, Mattapan, Roxbury, Jamaica Plain and any spot in between. But we didn't want ta give lives we wanted ta take'em.

After awhile people quit talkin bout how fucked up it was Ty was gone and how much they missed him. No more blowin' out smoke or pourin' out liquor in his memory. It seemed like everybody forgot. But my people never forgot, especially not me. As my team got stronger and money got longer, I needed a bigger connect. I talked ta Asan, the owner of John and Sham's. He turned me on to this cat named David from High Point. The deals he was comin' at me wit were too sweet ta pass up. Twelve a brick. There was nobody toppin that anywhere except my brother's connect. But you had ta buy like forty or fifty at a time. I was getting' it, but not like that, not yet anyway. So I decided to hoop up wit this cat for twenty of them things. We waited till Wednesday, a slow day, to make da deal.

I told him to meet me at the Brunswyck bowlin' lanes around twelve that afternoon. I didn't want to get got and I didn't want him feelin' that way either. So boom, I ride in da backseat of a tinted out Suburban wit like five of my people in their wit me. You do shit like that ta confuse niggas, cause they always think da head nigga's drivin or ridin shotgun.

Aight, so we pull up and I'm like way in the back, lookin out da window. I already know nigga's don't think like I do, cause they come in a big body Benz. So I can see right inta their shit. We parked in opposite directions, I did that for a reason.

I didn't want nobody but da driver ta get out on da side their car was on. You never know what might happen, plus I didn't want them seeing who was in da back. Everybody got out their car except their driver. That let me know that da driver was nothing more than that.

Everybody got out da Suburban except me and Diamond, who sat beside me. Pinero is O. G. status in this click, but I let my little man Cross, who was only 15 at da time handle da transaction. They thought he was jokin, till he showed them da money. Diamond had been about ta jump out da car when one of them moved too quick, but I stopped her and I pointed at a cat on da other side of da Benz. I told her that I was gonna kill him as soon as they got those bricks.

Diamond never questioned me, because she knew how I moved and everything had its reason. She knew I'd tell her in time. My heart was beating so fast, I thought I was gonna have a heart attack. Right there in front of my mothafuckin face was Diavante'. I don't know how I kept my composure. I wanted ta get this nigga so bad, I can taste it."

"Why didn't you?" Kenya asked, feeling the story out. "Because da timing wasn't right. I outnumbered him, but I didn't want it ta jump off like that. I wanted everything ta be perfect. So we made da deal and left. But all I can think was that someone had heard my cries. That it was my fate, my destiny, ta murk this nigga.

"A month went past before I had everything set up. I copped a few more bricks from him, so he wouldn't think nothing and would get careless. I made some calls back home and got an entourage ta come down after I noticed da number of Congrejoes poppin up. Come ta find out he had gained rank like me. So my boys, plus those from up da way were waiting on me. Their sole purpose was one thing and one thing only. To destroy every Congrejoes under Diavante' from da bottom up and leave that nigga ta me. It worked at first, almost too good. It seemed like they wanted ta get rid of da bottom soldiers ta see who were weak and who were survivors. But as we started getting closer to the top, I got locked. Come to find out this nigga named Drama...."

"Kiki cousin Drama?"

"Yeah, that's him. He had it made too. He was like one of da first people, after my first five that I put down. After da money started flowing he got greedy, so I got rid of him."

"Where he at now?"

"Dead and no I ain't do it," Solo quickly said. He wasn't lying. He didn't do it, but he was there to watch it be done. Still he wasn't gonna let Kenya know that.

"Anyway, come to find out, that nigga told David who was getting at him. Where my stash house was at and all. That's when da war was really took to da streets."

"Yeah, I remember that. People were scared to come out their house for like a month straight."

"I wouldn't've come out either. I had niggas poppin' at anybody wit gray on. Fa real. I had went into that fuck everybody mode. But no matter how many of them niggas got shot up, I never could find Diavante'. He must've seen how all his people were folding and he bounced again. But like any real G, he had a position ta hold so he couldn't go anywhere or his own fam would kill him. Then knowin me from when we were little, he knew what he was up against, but he couldn't hide forever. He didn't plan to either. I found out from someone that he paid this nigga to have me killed, but da bullet hit someone else and I ended up wit da murder charge. I was given a life sentence, but my appeal came through and my conviction was over turned.

"So what you gonna do now?"

"What kinda question is that? I'm a fine this nigga and put a hole in his ass. I can't sleep thinkin that my brother died in vain. I'm trying ta play soft hoping he'll stick his head out, especially since he done built his team up again."

"So what's this gotta do wit Splash?"

"I told you."

"And nothing's gonna change that?"

"Not a thing. And all I can say is tell him if he get in da way I'm sendin flowers," Solo said as he turned over indicating that he was through talking and wanted some sleep.

All Kenya could do was look at Solo. She hated to pick between him and her brother, but she knew it had to be done. She rolled over herself hoping that sleep would bring some sort of answer.

Solo never did go to sleep. He laid on his side staring at the wall as a tear rolled out of his eye. This was a tear of the pain caused from his brother's death. It was one of the reasons he didn't like to tell the story. The hate that had resurfaced as he told Kenya what happened was almost unbearable. He knew that killing Diavante' wasn't an option, it was a must. He had to do it for Sangres, his family and most importantly himself. This time he wanted to make sure he got it right.

He had a sixth sense for scooping out snakes and his radar had been buzzing a lot lately and he had only been home five months. He wondered about that nigga Drake and had he ever attempted what he told him to do. More than likely, no. He also felt like he was sleeping with the enemy and he probably fucked up by telling her about his initial beef with David. He only told it to close people, but she said she was pregnant, a little too pregnant. Two months ago meant that she got pregnant the first night that they had sex. So she had tricked him. Hah, he knew he couldn't get any sleep here, not tonight anyway.

Solo got up and went to the dresser and closet to grab some clothes to put on. He had started leaving clothes over here because he never knew when he'd stop by to stay the night.

"Where you going," Kenya murmured from under the covers.

"To get some air, I can't sleep," he said grabbing Precious and heading to the front door. He grabbed the garbage bag with his clothes in it and left.

Kenya didn't bother to stop him. She knew it'd be worthless, so she let him go and went back to sleep.

CHAPTER 12

Solo unlocked the door to the townhouse apartment and stopped short by what he saw. He made it a habit to stop by Kenya's crib at least once a day. He never came by at a specific time, because he was hoping to catch her doing something. Today, he didn't know what to make of what he was seeing right now. There were three girls sitting in the living room wearing a lot of revealing clothes. They all looked as good as Kenya if not better. He recognized one of them as Porsha. He thought of his man Clay and knew he'd love to see this. He figured the least he could do was take some pictures and send it to him.

"Hey baby," Kenya said taking attention off of her friends. She was still giving him his space, so that he had enough time to think about where they were going.

Solo watched as Kenya got up and made her way towards him. She had been showing more and more every week, making him doubt more and more about how long she said she was pregnant. He stiffened up a bit when she wrapped her arms around his neck and kissed him. He figured that she was letting her friends know who he was. It didn't matter, because he knew he could get anyone of them if he wanted to.

"Ooh, Kenya. You didn't tell us you had a stallion stored away."

"You didn't ask. Plus, you around a man of mine is a major no, no."

"Mmmmm, so this the one that be having you walking around like you been riding a horse?"

"Shut up Torri," Kenya said smiling.

"Hi, my names Torri," a Puerto Rican chick said standing up and putting her hand out. You could tell she was one of those girls who was used to having money. She was too pretty for her own good.

"Hold up T, this one's mine," Kenya quickly said, knowing that if you gave Torri the chance she'd be the first to prove your man was unfaithful.

"You better watch him, cause someone's gonna test him."

"Whatever. Solo, these are my girls. You already know Porsha and you just met Torri. That dark beauty over there wit the dreds is Jocelyn. Ya'll this is Solo."

"Hey Solo," Torri and Jocelyn said together. Porsha just looked at him.

"What up?" solo said putting the bags he still held in his hand on the floor.

"What you got?" Kenya asked looking down at the bags.

"Some things for my nieces."

"Oh."

"Ay yo, can ya'll do me a favor?" he asked looking at each of them.

"And what's that?" Jocelyn asked biting down on a fingernail trying to look sexy.

'Yeah, Solo thought, 'he could slide in one of these broads wit ease'. It was something about this group of women, that wasn't right. He had the impression that they were doing a lot of partner swapping or seeing who could fuck the other person's man first.

"I gotta man on lock right and I told him I'd send him some flicks of some females. But I ain't wanna send him none of just anybody. And ya'll about da best I've seen so far."

"We are da best you gonna see," Porsha threw in.

"You got dat right girl," Kenya said giving her da pound.

"And yes, we'll take da pictures if that's what you're asking," she said patting her hair and straightening her tennis skirt.

"Bet, I'll be right back," Solo said running upstairs, then coming back down with a Polaroid. In a way he felt like Hugh Hefner as he watched them stand in their sexiest poses. They were showing their ass, rubbing titties. Even pretending to kiss, but it didn't look to fake to him. It looked like they were used to doing this type of thing. Either they were trying to make sure his boy had some real exclusive flicks or were seeing who could turn him on the most. The more pictures he took, the less respect he had for any of them. Kenya included. He knew that it was all in good nature, but they were acting like those broads that be fucking for money at the bike rallies.

When he was finished, he walked off with a smile and went upstairs flipping the photos. His smile slowly faded as he kept flipping and flipping. He noticed that all of them had the same tattoo that he saw on Kenya their first night together. It took him a few seconds before it hit him where he had seen it before. While he was locked up his man Pharaoh had a picture of one of these girls, Torri to be exact, now that he thought about it. He told him that she was a part of this click, called the "Money Hungry Clit", that's what the initials stood for. 'A bunch of pussy hungry for money' was Pharaoh's exact words.

Now he knew what she meant by having a lot to offer. They probably were sharing each other's bed, but that he could care less about, cause he knew a lot of females who went both ways. Sometimes he encouraged women to do it. What he was concerned with was if Kenya thought she was gonna handle him like the next man.

"Yo, Kenya, come here for a second," he hollered downstairs, then sat on the bed holding the pictures.

When Kenya walked in the room the first thing she noticed was Solo's gun laying beside him and thought that 'that gun touched his dick more than she did.' "What's up baby?" she asked. Then cracked a smile when she seen him holding the pictures he just took. "I bet ya boy'll love those there."

"Yeah, he'll love 'em. He'll love dem tats too." Solo said looking at her to see what she was gonna say. He watched her smile start to fade and knew she was gonna try to talk her way out of this.

"I was gonna tell you," she said shutting the door, so the girls couldn't hear what was going on.

"It's been almost three months, what da fuck you mean you was gonna tell me? When after one of dem broads came throwin her pussy at me and let it slip out?"

"No," she said casting her eyes down.

"Then when Kenya, huh? I be layin' in dis bed telling you all types of personal shit and you up in my face everyday holdin' back I knew I couldn't trust you. Now all I wanna know is if you trying ta set me up or not?"

Baby, you know I would never do that," she said dropping to her knees in front of Solo. "I'm sorry. I knew I should a told you, but I got so caught up in us and the baby, I..."

"Man, fuck that baby shit," Solo hollered as he jumped up and slung the pictures at the wall. Kenya fell on her butt and stared up at him scared for the first time in his presence. She never seen him get this mad before. "Who da fuck you think you talking' to, huh? I've been doin' this shit all my life. Don't nobody forget about they click. And if you had forgot about'em they wouldn't be sitting downstairs. So you ca run that weak shit on somebody who doesn't know better, but don't come at me wit cause I ain't trying to hear it."

"Baby, I'm sorry. I know I was wrong, let me make it up to you," she sat back up and started running her hands up his thighs.

"Get da fuck off me yo. Ain't shit to make up this time yo," he said knocking her hands away from him.

"What the fuck you want from me then? Huh Solo?" she asked standing up. She was tired of being nice nice. This was the real Kenya. The one who had started and led the Money Hungry Clit.

"Tell me Solo. You want me to kiss ya feet, suck ya dick, what? Oh, you think I'm a go down there and tell my girls I can't lead them no more? You can forget it, cause that ain't gonna happen. I started this shit, so I'm livin it. You can except it or get out."

Solo picked up Precious and headed for the door, but was stopped by a hand on his arm. His reflexes were so quick that it caught Kenya off guard and before she could stop him, he had his hand around her throat. "Didn't I tell you not to touch me?

Now I oughta put my motha fuckin foot in ya ass, but that ain't what I'm about. You played me twice, I ain't gonna let you do it again."

"Get your hands off me."

"Or what? What you gonna do call ya little friends up here ta save you?"

"I can handle you myself."

"Is that right?" Solo asked. He already knew that she was feisty and liked being roughed up. It was a turn on for her, but this wasn't a time to play games. She had crossed him one too many times and the only thing he could do was cut her loose.

"Yeah that's right."

"Go 'head and try."

Kenya tried to break away, but the hold he had on her was like a vice grip. She thought to herself, that she had finally pushed him too far. "Oh, so you gonna kill me now?"

"If I wanted you dead, I would a done it a long time ago, like three weeks long."

"Fuck you nigga, you ain't nothing' but a big pussy waitin' ta get fucked."

"What bitch, Solo said raising Precious up so her and Kenya could do some kissing of their own. He saw her eyes grow to the size of quarters when he made the introduction. She started fidgeting when he cocked the hammer back and heard the piss hitting the floor when he pulled the trigger. When she jerked after hearing the click he let her go. He never did put a bullet in the chamber. He watched as she slumped down on the floor and let out a low chuckle.

"Bitch you ain't ready ta die."

"Get da fuck out," she said through trembling hands.
When he opened the door he saw Kenya's home girls ready to come through the door. "Fucking sluts," he said as he walked pass them.

"I'll be back for my stuff," he hollered out before leaving.

CHAPTER 13

"Man, I'm sick of this shit man. Look at these motherfuckers out here, Gorilla pimpin' da goddamn customers and shit. Lookin' like crack heads dem damn self. Word up P, it ain't like it use ta be, when it was just a few of us out here ya know?" Solo stated. He was riding shotgun in Pinero's '74 coupe Deville. Pinero who always trying to act like he was old school. They were riding through the strip on McConnell checking out the scenery and seeing what was jumping. Solo had finally copped a house to pump out of and put some workers in it. This was nothing new, it was how he use to roll before his bid. Making pick-ups and drop offs. Seeing if the customers were being treated right by his workers. It was easier this way, because he didn't have to worry about the police and begging fiends.

"Times done changed man. These little niggas nowadays wanna get pain. They hungry, but eat da wrong way. Plus, you got them New York cats comin down here tryin ta force feed these fiends and shit."

"That's why I be like fuck New York, I rep da Bean nigga. Don't get me wrong, I've ran into a few New York cats who be about they business and not on that bullshit. Ay, yo, check this out. Pull this shit over."

"For what?"

"Man, pull this shit over."

"Ya, ha, Bruh. What's da deal man, what's up?" Solo asked jumping out of the car and walking up to this guy he never seen before.

"What da fuck you mean what's up?" the guy said, who was tall, slim and dark skinned. He was pulling on the hair of Sarah, his moneymaker.

"Why you yanking on my girl like that."

"Nigga this ain't ya girl, I've been serving her for two years and I ain't seen you once, so don't come over here wit that bullshit."

"Nigga, I said that's my muthafuckin girl so raise da fuck up."

"That's Solo nigga, you better listen to him," Sarah said still trying to break the dude's grip.

"Bitch I don't give a fuck if that nigga name Duet, I run this shit and ain't nobody gonna do a motha...."

Before he could get the rest of the words out Solo punched him in his mouth, knocking him to the ground. "Man, what da fuck," he said touching his mouth to feel if it was bleeding or not.

"Yeah, now what were you sayin' nigga?" Solo asked pulling Precious out and putting it to the guy's head. This time the chamber was full.

"Come on man, it ain't even gotta be like that."

"Yo, Solo, chill man chill," Pinero said from behind pulling on his shoulder.

"Yo, Pinero, this ya peeps." The guy said still sitting on the ground.

"Yeah that's my man. Don't you recognize da colors nigga?"

"Why ya'll basin' on me for man, she owe me money."

"How much?" Solo asked

"Twenty."

"Nigga I'll beat da shit out you. I know Sarah and if she ain't worth a free twenty, then you don't need ta serve her," Solo went in his pocket and pulled out a knot of money. "Here nigga, here go forty, don't even serve her no more yo.

"And Sarah, go down Booker and you'll see a house wit a green flag on it. That's my spot now. I'm a tell my boys ta give you something, Aight?"

"Okay Solo," Sarah said fast walking up the street on her way to Solo's crack spot.

"And don't buy from no one else. Matter fact let everybody know that's where I'm at and don't come pass da bridge." Solo threw at Sarah's fleeing back, right before she jumped in on anonymous car. 'Damn, she don't waste no time' he thought.

"And you nigga, who you paying' dues to?"

"I got that Solo," P told him.

"Don't let me see you do that shit no more, or you can find another town ta hustle in. Let's go P."

"Damn my nigga. You really hate that shit don't you?" Pinero asked when they got back in his car.

"Hells yeah man. They ain't no different than you and me, they just got a serious habit. Why you think they be bringing' all their business to me first? Cause I treat'em like normal people. I've even took a few of'em out ta eat. Back in da day I use ta hand out coats in da winter. Little shit like that'll keep'em spendin wit you and you only. See I don't tell ya'll how ta run ya'll spots, but from Ray Warrant to dat bridge is me. I'm tellin you, now watch how that house I just opened up start boomin.'

"Who all in there?"

"Toby, John, Cash, Reno and Bobby."

"Damn, five niggas?"

"I got two runners, one cook, one server and a look out."

"You don't play do you?"

"Nope and I don't expect you or any of my OG's to either."

"Don't worry 'bout me, I'm handlin mine."

"We'll let da numbers tell. But yo, take me ta Kenya's crib. I gotta go get my shit from outta there."

"What's up wit ya'll?"

"I gotta cut her loose man. She too fuckin' sneaky for me you. I don't trust that bitch."

"Didn't you say she was pregnant?"

"Yeah, she pregnant, but I got my doubts about that too."

"You know her better than I do. How you get there my nig?"

"Take Wendover, it's faster."

"Yo, I'm tellin' you son. Boston gonna come through," Solo said getting out the car.

"Man, Boston ain't gonna do shit. Every year they go to da playoffs and can't get pass da second round," Pinero shot back as he cut the car off and followed Solo.

"As soon as Pierce and Walker get some help. My niggas going get us another ring."

"You mean as soon as them niggas learn how ta pass that rock."

"Whatever, yo, Hold up. I hear somebody," Solo said when he got the door open.

"Probably one of her friends."

"She ain't got no friends. No male friends anyway," he crept in the house with Pinero right behind him. He knew if anything jumped off, he'd be right with him helping him fight. Solo heard Kenya's voice coming from the dining room talking to somebody about a baby. All he could think of was how many ways this broad had let him down. He walked through the doorway ready to set things straight, but stopped short. Sitting at the table across from Kenya was Splash.

"What da fuck this nigga doin' here?" he asked grilling Splash with burning eyes.

"I told him to come over. Plus, I didn't think you were comin' back."

"I told you I was comin back for my stuff. Don't even worry bout it. It ain't gon take me but five minutes anyway. He turned and went upstairs with Pinero behind him.

"What's up my nigga? You trying to get rid of that mothafucka or what?"

"I told Drake to handle that."

"Man, where you at Yo? You know Drake ain't gon do shit. Plus, Kase and Chaos ain't seen that nigga since you told him ta do that."

"What else they say?"

"Oh, he definitely Congrejo or work for'em."

"You find out who brought that nigga?"

"Carlos."

"We can't do it here, it ain't da right place."

"You know I'll murk that nigga anywhere. I've been waiting ta get him for da longest.

"I'll tell you what, after we leave here, drop me off at my grandma's house and you can do what you want."

"However you want it my nigga. So that's da green light right?"

"Yeah that's da green light."

"Bet." Pinero said feeling his adrenaline pump. His beef with Splash was parallel to Solo's and David's. He didn't know if he could wait till he dropped Solo off, but he had to respect his superior's wishes or face the consequences.

When they finished, they walked back downstairs. Solo told Pinero to put his stuff in the car while he gave Kenya her key back.

"So this is it huh? You just gonna walk out on me and da baby?" Kenya asked when he put the key down in front of her.

"That shit ain't mine yo,"

"What da fuck you mean it ain't yours?"

"Just like I said. It ain't mine."

"Then whose is it? Huh? Tell me that."

"Nah, you tell me."

"Fuck that nigga Kenya. You don't need him," Splash threw in.

"Nigga, you better watch ya fucking' mouth. "Cause you ain't even supposed to be breathin' right now. And how I'm feelin I can put a bullet in both you and this bitch."

"I don't know who you talkin to like that, but it can't be me." Splash said getting up.

"Nigga you got five seconds to back da fuck up."

"Or what?" Splash was the cocky type and didn't care if he had to shoot you or cut you, because he was nice with a gun or a knife. He knew that Solo wasn't by himself, but he never used being out numbered as an excuse to get at somebody. What he didn't know was that the person with Solo was Pinero, who was what they called a real gun clapper.

When Splash made that last statement, Solo hooked off on him, knocking him into the wall. He saw when Splash pulled his gun out and realized that this was the one time that he left his behind. A loud explosion shook the wall as he fell to the floor. He didn't feel any type of burning so he knew he wasn't hit. He looked up and saw Splash with a hole in his chest oozing with blood. Pinero stepped through the dining room doorway with a Desert Eagle smoking in his hand.

"That nigga just couldn't wait could he?" Pinero said looking over at Splash, who was taking his last breaths, because he didn't have the energy to do anything else.

Kenya got up and started screaming 'Oh God'. They sounded much different than the ones she was screaming three months ago.

"Let's go before the cops come," Solo said getting off the floor and heading to the front door.

"I'm a get you motherfuckers, I swear," Kenya shouted after them.

Solo never looked back one time, this part of his life was over and he didn't think twice about leaving it behind. As they drove off, they passed neighbors, who just had to be nosy and knew that this would be the last time Pinero would be driving around in this car.

Pinero drove with a Colgate smile on his face, like a black joker. He didn't care about the car, because he had planned on getting a newer model anyhow. The only thing that kept running through his mind was that he had finally got that nigga.

CHAPTER 14

That night Solo laid low at one of the lower Sangres' house. He wasn't sure if Kenya told the police anything or not. But he wasn't gonna take the chance by going over anyone's house that she knew about.

He knew he couldn't stay holed up like this and thought about Shakim. He looked through his cell numbers till he came to the one of Hakim's that Miss Rose gave him. When he dialed the number he thought that he wouldn't get an answer. After five rings his brother picked up.

"Hello?"

"It's me, yo."

"Who's me?"

"Solo."

"Oh, what up bruh?"

"That offer still open about me comin' down there?"

"Why, what's up? What you done done?"

"I done nothing, I just need to get away from this shit for a minute."

"When you tryin' to leave?"

"In two days. I gotta let some people know and make sure everything's straight."

"Aight, I'll call da airport."

"Don't worry bout that. I can handle it, just be at that airport to pick me up aight?"

"Aight. Man, call me before you leave."

"Aight yo, one."

"One."

Solo hung up his phone and laid back on the couch he was taking up. He felt out of place, but it was either that or risk going to jail for a real murder or accessory to one. Still he couldn't stay still, so he got up and went in the bedroom and woke up Charlotte, the girl whose house he was at. She was under Diamond and had been around for a while. It wasn't anything new for one of the male Sangres to drop by either her crib or one of the other female's cribs.

But to see Solo standing at her door wasn't normal. Still she let him in the same. She felt that she had no choice, being that he was there leader and all.

"Charlotte," Solo whispered shaking the body underneath the covers. "Charlotte, wake up."

"Huh? What? What's up?" she asked not liking that she was brought out of her slumber.

"I need you ta do me a favor."

"What time is it?"

"It ain't even twelve yet."

"I need you ta call this number for me."

"What number?"

"This girl named Kenya. Call and see if she put da police on me."

Solo sat down on the edge of the bed and waited for Charlotte to get fully awake. He watched as she sat up and cut on the lamp on her nightstand. Wiping her mouth she picked up the phone and he told her the number. As they waited for an answer they stared at each other over the space between them. He saw the roundness of one of her loose breast under the t-shirt she wore.

She started to blush but quickly snapped straight as she started speaking into the phone. He could hear Kenya's voice come through the phone. A lot bitches and other words were exchanged before she slammed the phone down.

"Stupid bitch."

In any other situation Solo would've been laughing, but this was a serious matter. Still, he admired the way she handled herself and knew why Diamond had took her in.

"What she say?"

"She said you got other people to worry about than da police. She said she don't want them ta interfere wit what was gonna happen to you and Pinero."

"That all?"

"Yeah, besides her runnin her mouth. If need be I can round up some girls and…"

"Nah, don't worry bout it. Her time'll come."

"I know if I see her it's over."

"In da mornin I'm a need you ta drop me off at da crib. Aight?"

"Yeah, okay. Are you aight?"

"Yeah, I'm straight. I'll let you go back to sleep."

"You can't sleep on that couch can you?"

"Nah, not really. I done got so used to sleepin' wit somebody beside me it doesn't feel right."

"You ca sleep in here. I don't mind.

"I don't wanna invade your space like that."

"That's aight, as long as you don't try nothin'."

Solo didn't say another word as he kicked his shoes off and put Precious on the nightstand. Cutting the lamp off, he slid under the covers next to Charlotte. He kept on all of his clothes, out of respect for her, but didn't feel out of place by throwing an arm around her waist. "You don't mind do you?"

"I don't know, Solo."

"Don't worry. I can't penetrate through all this denim."

"If you say so, but da first time you do somethin you hittin da couch."

"Bet," he agreed. "Charlotte, how long you been wit us?"

"'Bout five goin' on six years."

"So you was there when that war jumped off?"

"Yup."

"So you like da first person she brought?"

"Second, Qiana was first. No, my fault I was third, Qiana was first and Karen was second. I keep forgettin she was there before me."

"Nah, you right Karen use ta be around but she never got down until Qiana came through or should I say stopped comin through?"

"So, I was second."

"Yeah, cause I be knowin who were da first troopers cause there weren't that many then. Matter fact there weren't no females till I put Diamond down. After I got locked though, niggas act like they forgot da rules of bringin somebody."

"If you know why'd you ask me?"

"Cause, I do that. Ta see what people'll say. That's how I feel'em out. Some'll lie and try to make themselves bigger than they are. But you. Yeah, I remember you. You used to have that little backpack purse joint. And had your hair done like da Brat."

"Yup, that was me too."

"Tell me somethin. You ain't got no man runnin up in here?"

"Yeah, but he been on da block for like three days straight."

"Who you talkin bout?"

"Charles."

"Charles. Charles. Do I know him?"

"I don't know. I believe so. He da one killed Sebastian back in '94."

"Oh that Charles, he got manslaughter and ended doin like what five years?"

"Yup."

"Damn, you fuckin' wit a live wire ain't you?"

"He done calmed down since he got shot."

"Oh yeah. Who brought him?"

"I took him to da Twins."

"I shoulda figured that, he fit into how they get down to a T. Where he at now?"

"On South St. He said he trying ta prove he ca handle business. He tryin ta move up to second string."

"I'll holla at Kase and them see if we ca get that nigga ta come home more often."

"What about you?"

"What you mean?"

"Why you be messin wit them other broads, when you got someone waitin on you?"

"Who dat?"

"Act like you don't know," she said turning her head to look at him.

"Who Diamond?"

"Yeah, Diamond, that girl love you to death, but you keep ignorin her."

"Diamond knows where we stand. She like a sister to me."

"She like, but she ain't. Who you think took care of you while you were locked up?"

"Not ya'll that's for sure. My grandma da one who held a nigga down."

"Errnt, wrong answer. Three fourths of what ya grandma sent you came from her. She just had your grandma put her name on it."

"Why didn't she say somethin'?"

"Cause she ain't da type ta run around tellin or tryin to explain what she do. You probably would've told her to stop and take care of business.

"Damn, I wish I would've known."

"She ain't tryin ta have you, because she held you down, she want you there cause you really love her. She damn near came a bum for your ass."

"How you figure that, wit all ya'll out here?"

"You must don't know her that well then. Cause Diamond ain't wit no handouts. If she can't do it or get it on her own, she won't fuck wit it."

"What's that gotta do wit being a bum?"

"She cleared out her account ta make sure them sorry ass lawyers of yours got you back on da streets."

"Now I know you bullshittin, my money was long. I went broke payin dem motherfuckers."

"Your money ran out."

Solo stopped to think about everything that was just revealed to him. He knew that Diamond cared, but he didn't think it was that serious. Maybe what he wanted and needed had been staring him in the face for close to seven years. His queen, a real queen. The piece he was missing. He had put her in the position of a measly knight, separating them by two snakes. He had always considered it, the only female O.G. in his click. Now he knew and Charlotte confirmed it. He pulled up the board.

Kenya and Trish were automatically knocked out the way. He quickly put Diamond in her hard earned spot. Who he was gonna get to fill the other spaces up was a toss up. More than likely he'd get a pick from Diamond and the Twins.

Not another word had been spoken and Charlotte took advantage of the silence by dozing off. Solo wasn't too far behind. He felt at ease knowing that a missing piece of his puzzle was finally found. The image of him and Diamond was burned in his mind as he drifted off to sleep.

CHAPTER 15

Cross had taken after Solo so much that he drove around like him. He was young, but grown of the same time. He'd be 21 in December, only three months away and he was ready. What little things he didn't learn from Solo, in the short time they spent together before his bid he learnt from Diamond. He trusted her schooling because he knew that what she taught him came from Solo. He considered himself a business man. He had him a small clothing store in the Downtown area on the corner of South Elm and Lee St. named North South Fashions. He had a business license so everything was legit.

While most people his age were getting ready to graduate from college, he was making plans to graduate from one store to two stores, from five figures to six. The money he made on the streets he funneled into his business, advertisement and promotion. So when the cops came sniffing they'd smell nothing but roses. So riding around in his green candy painted Avalanche he had not a fear in the world, but he knew there was a problem. It was a problem that needed his wit or maybe there wasn't a problem at all, just some bonding that wanted to be done. But he doubted that that was the reason his passenger seat was being occupied by his mentor.

"How's da business?" Solo asked scrunched down in his seat with his hat cocked over his eyes. When Charlotte dropped him off, he took a shower and threw on a dark green sweat suite with matching Air 1's and fitted Oakland A's hat. Then he called up Cross to come get him.

"Which one?"

"Both."

"I'm working on opening another store on Market St. across from A&T so they won't have ta go all da way to da mall ta get some hot gear. That other thing, I got Joy and Shawn out there, you know they got a baby together. So it looks like a regular ol' family that livin in da house they pumpin out of."

"How's it goin, are they straight?"

"Man, it's a gold mine out there. You know da police ain't thinkin' drugs in da neighborhood they would live in."

Solo's phone rang and he quickly answered it.

"Yo... They found him? What happened? What they do wit him? ... Good, Good... Aight... Aight I'll holla," he hung up.

"Who was that?"

"P, he said da Twins found that nigga Drake."

"Oh, word. What they do wit him?"

"Took him down to Anson County."

"What's down there?"

"Some big ass catfish."

Cross shook his head, glad that he wasn't the one to ever become a victim of Solo's wrath. "I heard about what happened yesterday, is everything straight?"

"Nah. She said she ain't goin' to da police. But now I got to worry about who she goin to or how she comin. That's one thing she promised ta get Pinero and me. She got her own little crew. I don't know how deep, that ain't my concern. It's about goin against the Congrejoes before I'm ready."

"You know we out number them three to one on all sides of town."

"It don't matter. You should know that da man who uses his head always stays in front. Yo, go to da Dustbowl."

"What's over there?"

"Some business I need you to handle."

"Me?"

"Yeah, you. Don't you wanna get a promotion or you happy where you at? You about to turn 21 and you'll be of age."

"You serious."

"You know I don't play when it comes to this."

"What you want me to do?"

"What are da rules of bringin' someone?"

"Five months of research and groomin ta make sure they're official and ready."

"And if you bring in a snake?"

"Murder."

Solo said no more as they reached the Dustbowl. He had Cross pull up right in front of the park and saw about nine Sangres posted around. Since looking out others making deals, it reminded him of the movie "Clockers." He saw Carlos sitting at a picnic table playing rummy. "Yo, Carlos, come here man," he said sticking his head out the window so he could see who was calling him.

As he watched Carlos get up and head his way, he saw Cross lift up the armrest and pull out a Glock 19. Tucking it in his pants as he got out the truck. He went around to the passenger side and leaned against the hood of the truck near the window and waited. 'Damn this boy don't play,' Solo thought holding back a smile.

"Yo, what up Cross? What up Solo?" Carlos was a short stocky man that looked Mexican.

"What up Lossy Los. I see you got a little team out here.

"Yeah a little somethin'"

"They all under you?"

"Yeah, I brought'em in."

"Tell'em to come here."

"All of'em?"

"Yeah, why not. I outta know who reppin my shit right?"

"Yeah, you right about that," he said turning around and calling everybody over.

"Yo, ya'll meet Solo. He da head dog over all Sangres."

"What up little homies. Ya'll tell me something'. How long Carlos wait before he gave ya'll a flag?" he listened to their answers. When none of them said five months, he looked at Carlos who was fidgeting. "What's wrong Los? You know da rules right?"

"I'm saying' I needed some people and I don't trust nothing but family."

"I understand. You know a cat named Drake?"

"Yeah, I know Drake. I ain't seen him in a minute though."

"You ain't gonna see him either. He dead."

"Why? What he do?"

"Drake was a Congrejo."

"Nah, man."

"Yeah, man. Ya see why you suppose to wait five months. You break da rules Los and you have ta have justice served."

"I'm sayin what I gotta do?"

"Nothin. What are you?"

"Second string."

"So you've put in enough work to know better. My boy Cross here, Los been in this thing for seven years, he should be on O.G. he's put in so much work. But what are you?"

"I'm third rate."

"Third rate. Seven years and only third rate. That's because he wants to know every angle there is so he doesn't make any mistakes. Feel me? But guess what? Today he says he's ready ta move up to O.G. I told him an O.G. has ta be responsible, set things in order when they get out of hand. He says he's ready for that so boom here we are.

Are ya'll payin attention ta this?" he asked looking at the nine homies standing around. "This nigga broke da rules, now O.G. Cross is gonna set things straight." As soon as he got the words out of his mouth Cross pulled out his Glock and shot the back of Carlos' head off then briskly walked back to the driver side.

"Let that be a lesson learned ya'll. Follow da rules and you'll have nothin ta worry about. Don't even worry bout him. Leave him there. Any money you make, keep. I'm a send O.G. Kase over here ta show ya'll how to be real G's aight. Aight salute," he said throwing the Sangres sign up as they pulled away. "My boy, you O.G. now. Can you handle it?"

"Yeah, I got it."

"You'll have ta lay low now and get rid of this," he said referring to the Avalanche.

"Aight."

"Yo, take me over Diamond's crib."

When they got to Diamond's crib, Cross dropped him off and left to get rid of his truck. As soon as he got to the front door it opened up. Diamond stood there staring at him.

"What's up?" he asked walking in.

"Nothin are you aight?" she asked standing in some dark green sweat pants and T-shirt.

"Yeah, I'm straight."

"Where's Pinero at?"

"Still doin him."

"He ain't layin low?"

"Nah, he aight though, da police don't know nothin," he said sitting down in her laz-e-boy chair.

"How you know?"

"I called her."

"You need ta be careful wit bitches like her," Diamond said going into the kitchen.

"Yeah, I know. That's why I'm through wit her."

"Are you?" she asked trying not to show her happiness.

"Yup, that's how Splash ended up getting' killed. All I wanted ta do was get my stuff and go, but he had to open his mouth."

"You shoulda known that nigga wasn't gonna keep quiet. Here, I know you thirsty." She said handing him a bottle of Mystic strawberry/kiwi, then sat down on her couch.

"He shoulda known that I had Pinero wit me or he'd be alive. But I'm glad I had that nigga there or I'd a been dead."

"Why you say that?"

"Cause when that nigga went to shoot me, I realized I left my gun in P's car."

"I don't know what to say about you sometimes."

"As long as it's nothin bad, say what you like." He heard his phone go off then made a show of looking at the caller id, which he never did before. When he saw that the number belonged to Keisha, he handed the phone to Diamond. "Here answer this."

"Who is it?"

"My sister's friend. Tell her I can't come to da phone right now."

"I ain't."

"Damn, just do it."

Diamond answered the phone not once taking her eye off of Solo. After she said what he told her to, she took the phone from her ear. "She said it's important."

All Solo could think of was her trying to say she was pregnant and he wasn't trying to hear that. "Tell her I'll call her back."

"She said it has ta do wit Miss Rose."

"Give me that phone," he said grabbing the phone away from Diamond. "Yo, this better be some real serious shit."

"Shay been tryin ta call you all day. We at da hospital."

"Somethin wrong?" "What happened?"

"Miss Rose's been in a car wreck."

"What? Is she aight?" he asked getting up to pace around the living room.

"I don't know she's in surgery."

"Give me your car keys," he said to Diamond. "I'm on my way, which hospital?"

"Moses Cone."

"What's wrong, Solo?"

"Gimme ya goddamn keys."

"I'll be there in five minutes," Solo said hanging up his phone grabbing the keys out of Diamond's hand. He couldn't hear a word coming out of her mouth as he got into her car and sped off.

"I need ta know what floor Miss Gloria Rose is on? She was a car wreck victim."

"And who would you be sir?"

"Her grandson."

"That'll be on the third floor sir, but she's in surgery."

Solo didn't bother to wait on an elevator. He shot up the side stairs climbing four at a time. When he got to the third floor he saw Keisha rocking Shay back and forth. "Shay, Shay."

"Solo," Shay said getting up teary eyed and falling into Solo's arms.

"What's going on, How she doing?"

"They say she might not make it. She got crushed between two trucks."

"Calm down, everything's gonna be alright. Grandma's a trooper she'll pull through." Keisha take Jade and Quana ta ya house, me and Shay'll stay here."

"Okay," Keisha said taking Jade and Quana by the hand and leading them off.

After about an hour a doctor came out with a solemn look on his face. Solo was the first one to jump up. "Doc, what's up? Talk ta me."

"We can't save her, she's lost too much blood. There's internal bleeding that we can't stop."

"What da fuck you mean you can't stop it. You a doctor ain't you?"

"I've done everything I could do. I come out here to ask to end it right now or drag her along."

"What's that suppose ta mean?"

"She has about an hour and a half before her heart stops from lack of blood and in turn her brain shuts down, because there's no oxygen getting to it."

"Can we talk to her?"

"I don't know if she'll be able to hear you. She's unconscious."

"It doesn't matter. Just wake her up long enough to know we were there."

"Alright, if you wish."

They followed the doctor into the surgery room and could see where they had opened her up to stop the bleeding. Solo went over to where his grandmother was and grabbed her hand.

"Grandma, it's me Solomon, do you hear me. It's ya baby boy. Please don't leave me without talkin to me." Miss Rose was already gone or close to letting go, but somehow summed up enough energy to open her eyes. She cut her eyes to Shay then Solo and cracked a weak smile.

"They finally got me huh? The spirits must feel my job is done now it's up to you. You da last one.

Take care of ya sista cause she gon need you. Shay make sure them babies of yours are raised right."

"Grandma don't go," Shay cried.

"I've been ready for this for a long time ta get out of this cruel world. Solo that girl Diamond, you need" She started to say before coughing and going into convulsions.

"Grandma I love you," Solo said kissing her hand. Those were the last words Miss Rose heard before giving her life up.

Solo heard the loud beep from the flat line of the EKG and slowly stood up. He walked out of the room in a different world. He was numb to all outside noise. There wasn't a tear shed as he left the building, got in Diamond's car and went home.

CHAPTER 16

It was like his world was over. Nothing else mattered. He was numb to everything but the memories that were floating in his head. He had been up for two days straight sulking over his loss. Not getting up off of his bed to answer the phone or door. He paid attention to nothing, because right now he was still in a world where his grandmother was still alive. He didn't pay it no mind when the cab pulled into his driveway, nor did he hear his front door open and close.

When Diamond first heard what happened she became deeply concerned, but knew that Solo needed his space. After two days of not seeing him, she knew there was a problem. His sister had got in contact with her and told her he was at home, but wouldn't answer the door. She wanted to say just go in, but forgot that her and his grandma were the only one with a key. The first thing she noticed when she came in was that thick smell of weed smoke. It wasn't nothing new, but for someone that was by himself, it was. She went through each room looking for him. He wasn't in the dining room, but she could see in the kitchen where unwashed dishes were piled in the sink. She walked over to the sink and loaded the dishes into the dishwasher, then proceeded to the bedroom.

When she walked into the bedroom, she saw Solo sitting on his with his back to the wall. In his lap was a photo album. One in particular showed a group photo of him, Miss Rose, his mother and brother Tyrone. There were liquor bottles scattered on the floor and a blunt burning beside his leg. He probably drunk himself to sleep and smoked himself awake. She looked at his disheveled clothes and the half a head of loose cornrows and wanted to cry herself. It took her a while to realize that he didn't even know she was standing there.

"Solo", she whispered.

Solo heard his name being called and thought it was coming from the picture in his lap, until he heard again. He looked in the direction of the voice and saw Diamond standing there.

"Go away, leave me alone," he said in a muffled voice.

"No. I won't go. People are worried about you and you're not making things no better by sittin here drinkin and smokin yaself ta def."

"Fuck what they think. What do they know? They don't care about me."

"I care about you," she said. "Here give me that," she grabbed Precious and put her on the dresser. She took the burning blunt out of his hand and put it out. Then started picking up the bottles. When she was finished, she went in the kitchen and came back with a glass of grapefruit juice.

"Here drink this. You look like you haven't slept in two days."

"I haven't." Solo said feeling himself coming back to life a little bit, but was still under the influence of the weed he had been smoking earlier and the bottle of Paul Masson he just finished.

"Well you need to get some, so you can be focused enough to handle these situations."

"What situations?" he asked, stopping her when she went to grab the photo album.

"Whatever might occur," she said locking eyes with him, and then felt the release of the album. She started taking his clothes off so he could get in bed. She had done this plenty of times before when he had gotten too drunk to do it himself.

"Charlotte told me what you did," he said watching her with admiration.

"And what was that?"

"How some of that stuff my grandma sent me in prison came from you. And about the lawyers too."
Diamond sighed,

"Charlotte talks too much."

"Why didn't you tell me?"

"Because I didn't want ta step on any toes."

"Come on D, you know that's some bullshit. You thought I'd turn you away."

"I didn't want to pressure you, because of da situation. Nor did I want ...never mind."

"You didn't want me to what? Come to you because you took care of me? Is that it?"

"Yeah, something like that. I don't wanna talk about it." She said walking out the room.

Solo sat in the darkness that enveloped him and could still feel the weight on his heart.

He didn't know if it would ever come off, but he knew that there was someone who at least loved him as much as his grandmother. When Diamond came back in the room she cracked a window to let the smoke haze clear up and picked up his removed clothes. Not once did Solo take his eyes off of her. He looked at the baggy jeans and sweatshirt and thought back to the first night he met her. That was the last time he seen her in anything revealing. Then the thought of his grandma hit him and tears burnt into the back of his eyes. Diamond glanced at Solo lying there and heard the sniffle noise he made. She quickly went to his side.

"What's wrong?" she asked sitting on the bed.

"She's gone. They took her away from me."

"No, don't cry. She's still here just not in the physical."

"I never even thanked her for being there for me, since my mother passed."

"Don't dwell on the bad stuff. Just think of all the good times you had together."

"You won't leave me will you? You and my sister are all I got."

"I won't leave you."

"Not even tonight?" he asked sitting up to look directly at her.

"Not even tonight."

Solo leaned forward to kiss her, but she pulled back.

"No, don't."

"What's wrong?"

"I don't want to mess up our friendship."

"I had stopped wantin' ta be your friend since I put you down."

"Then why didn't you say somethin'?"

"I figured that that was how you wanted it."

Diamond let go of a tear of her own as she listened to Solo talk.

"What's wrong?"

"All these years I've been holdin' back, watchin' you run around wit all these women envyin them. Wonderin why you never approached me like that. And you tellin me that all I had to do was say I wanted to be more than friends?"

"And I would've dropped whoever for you, wit no hesitation."

"What about now?"

"It's whatever you wanna do."

"Diamond didn't say no more as she stood up and took off her clothes, at the same time staring at Solo through the dark space. When she finished she started to get under the covers.

"Wait," Solo said getting gout of the bed. "I can't do this."

"What you mean..."

"I gotta go wash. I haven't showered in two days," he said dashing across the hall into the bathroom.

Diamond lay back in the bed and wondered if this was just another one of her dreams. Were she and Solo actually going to be together or was this just a reaction to his loss? She had been around Solo long enough to know when he was serious or not. And even with the ill situation, she knew he was for real about them if she wanted it to be that way.

With that thought on her mind she got out of the bed and headed to the bathroom.

Solo stood with his hands on the shower tile as if he was holding the wall up. He let the water run through the rest of the hair he had taken, as he thought about what he was doing. If it was anybody else he would've just mashed them out and send him or her on their way, but Diamond wasn't just anybody. She was like an untouched wife, who had been waiting. Waiting for over eight years to be exact. He was hoping that he wasn't making a mistake by taking things to another level with her. He was so deep in thought that he didn't notice anyone in the shower with him till he was touched on his shoulder. He reacted so fast that Diamond jumped herself.

Solo just stood there taking in the lovely sight in front of him. He wondered why he waited so long to see what lay underneath all those clothes she wore. He looked at her eyes that betrayed her innocence. The small nose, inviting mouth. Her body was very toned like an athlete's, with firm but thick thighs. He even peeped at her size five feet. Again the thought of perfection came to mind, but he didn't want to dwell on it. Because his dislikes might be someone else's likes and vice versa. With that in mind he put his hand up to the side of her head and ran it through the cornrows that fell to the middle of her back.

When their lips first touched, something came over Solo. All he wanted to do was devour Diamond. Dropping to his knees, he threw her right leg over his shoulder and went to work. Being that she hadn't been touched in so long, she came hard and fast.

Putting one hand on the top of his and the other on the wall, it was like she was trying to climb up the shower stall. As he stood up, he stopped to kiss her breast and lips. Then in one swift move he picked her up by her thighs and wrapped them around his waist. He used the back of the stall to support her as he slid in her. He could feel the tightness of her walls as he inched into her. He knew she was far from a virgin, but neglect can make you feel like one. So when she bit into his shoulder, after he was all the way in her, he didn't feel it. By that time, he had zoned out.

Diamond knew it had been a while, had actually forgot how it was and could feel every bit of Solo in her. When he started ramming into, not hard, but enough to say it was too much. She thought it was because she bit him. But when she leaned back and seen the water in his eyes, that didn't come from the showerhead, she knew that it wasn't the bite that was behind it. He was releasing a lot of tension that had been building inside him for years. If it was to be anyone who understood him, it was she. She just hoped he'd love her as much as she loved him.

Solo sat under a canopy listening to the pastor quote some passing verses. On his right sat Diamond and Shaneka was on his left, with Jade beside her. Quana was on his lap. He was dressed in all black like the rest of the mourners on this sad day. There was about a hundred people who attended the funeral.

Besides family, he didn't think that there was that many people Miss Rose associated with. He stood up to toss his bundle of roses on top of the casket as they lowered it into the ground. She was being buried next to his mother. When he turned to leave he saw Shakim standing under a tree. Even though it was drizzling outside he had on the darkest shades he could find. They were to hide the last tears he would shed for anyone.

"How long you been standin there?" he asked Shakim when he got up on him.

"Da whole time," he answered looking like a bigger version of Solo, minus the cornrows.

"You could've sat down."

"I didn't wanna be that close. I'm still in denial."

"I know what you mean. I believe you got some company," Solo said when Quana and Jade came running towards him followed by Shay and Diamond.

"Hey, stranger," Shay said when she got close, giving Shakim a jug and kiss.

"What's going on?"

"You ok Solo?" she asked.

"Yeah, I'm good," he answered putting his arm around Diamond. "Yo, Sha, this Diamond. Diamond this my brother Shakim, da stow away."

Shakim gave his acknowledgement with a handshake, but you could see he felt out of place not knowing if it was from his absence or just being back in NC.

"So what you gonna do now go back to Atlanta?" Shay asked.

"I probably won't leave till tomorrow, me and Solo if you still trying to come down."

"Yeah, I'm still comin. I gotta get away from this shit for a few weeks." He said, looking down at Diamond waiting for her to complain.

"Don't worry 'bout me. I'll be aight till you get back," Diamond said letting him know that nothing had changed with her. She could still hold her own. She was also happy when he bent down to kiss her showing his affection for her in public. This let her know that what he said about them being together wasn't just words.

Shay had to do a double take at what she saw, which was something her brother never did out in the open. It was like a family thing to never kiss and tell. He must really care for that girl to do that in front of us, she thought to herself. But she knew that, if anybody was perfect for him it was Diamond, despite the fact that she turned him on to Keisha.

All she could say was about time and realized too late that she had spoken it out loud. "My bust," she said when she saw Diamond blush.

"Ya'll trying to go mingle wit our lovely family?"

"I don't know what for, they don't give a fuck about us, not me anyway. I'm da black sheep of da family remember."

"Boy shut up."

"What? I'm serious. Fuck it, I guess I can go get some of that ol' good Pett cookin I ain't had in about six years. See how much these mothafuckas miss a nigga," he said heading to where they were holding the reception with Diamond under his arm and umbrella shielding them.

"That boy ain't changed a bit," Shakim said following behind him.

"Oh, he's changed. This right here done it. We might not see it, but I know. Ain't no more love in that boy heart. And da only way I see it different is if that girl puts it there."

"Why you say that?" Shakim asked stopping.

"First he loses Ty and you know how much he loved that nigga. Then Ma, now grandma? That's too much for one person ta handle."

"We loss'em too."

"But not like he did. Ty died in his arms. Ma, while he was locked up for something he didn't do. He's hurt cause he never got da chance to really spend time with her like we did and he never told her he loved her. The same with Miss Rose. He feels guilty about all their deaths."

"He has us."

"It's not the same. You in Atlanta. You probably haven't even sent him a card, money, or nothin, huh? I ain't no better. I haven't been around since he was fourteen, but I did send him a card every now and then and some money. When he got locked up both times. Still too much time away severed our bond. Oh, he loves us, but not like them. And I believe that girl is the only one he will ever deeply love again."

"Who is she?"

"When I came down here the first time I saw her she was giving' grandma some money to send to him. Then she'd come by every so often either to drop something off for Solo or to just talk. It took me a while after seeing all that green every time she came over, who she was. She da reason he out today."

"For real?"

"Yup. Spent all her money on them greedy ass lawyers of his. She really loves him too."

"So she's more than just another broad huh?"

"It took her awhile to get him to notice her, but after what I seen today, she finally got him. And after all she's done and rollin wit him for over eight years, I'd have to say she's more than another broad. I'd say she's more like his queen."

"Yo, ya'll comin or what?" Solo hollered after his siblings. When he noticed them not behind him when he got to the reception hall door.

"I guess we better get goin. Don't wanna upset our baby brotha," Shakim said walking off.

CHAPTER 17

"I'm not feelin dat beat there man. Gimme dat last joint you played yo. Da one with da girl oohin behind da beat," Solo said into the microphone. "Yeah, that one. Cut out da light, I'm bout ta vibe ta this."

Shakim watched his brother through the booth's glass window. Even with the lights out he could still see him bobbing his head. "Tell me when you ready bruh."

"I was born ready."

"You on then," he said pressing the record button.

"Yo, yo, yo. What is there left/ why are you savin' my breath/ is it a promise you kept, break it/ nights I've slept naked/ days I've wept hate it/ I don't wanna be da one that makes it/ da only one that faces it/ da fact that you gone/ I might mourn today/ But tomorrow I might give up all reasons to pray/ just knowin that you gone...."

Shakim sat and listened to the emotions pouring out of Solo's mouth and new that he was speaking from the heart. He knew that this wasn't something that he took time to write.

Which made what he was saying more meaningful and felt. He also knew that he was talking to those he had lost. They had gone to Shakim's studio the day after they arrived in Atlanta. Solo was anxious telling him how he could flow and what not. Shakim asked to hear something, but Solo was like only in the studio. Shakim thought he was bullshitting till now. After Solo finished, he cut the lights back on.

"Yo, that was some heat. I got some other beats, you wanna try 'em out?"

"Bring 'em," Solo said feeling himself.

They went on like that all day. Shakim couldn't believe the energy Solo was giving off. He came full force on every track and made love to the beat. He knew that most of them were written, but it was still a fit. By the time Solo said he was through, they had thirteen tracks. Shakim figured that after he mixed them down and cleaned them up a bit, he'd have a pretty good CD.

"What you think?" Solo asked coming into the mixing room.

"I ain't think you had it in you."

"Man, I told you I don't be playin'"

"What you tryin to do wit that?"

"What you mean?"

"You tryin' to make that into a demo or what? Cause you got some straight fire on there now."

Solo could hear his songs playin back as the engineer worked the control buttons. He knew that what he just spit was better than a demo." Nah, I'm a drop that for twelve a pop."

"I figured that what you say. Cause I know where you can get a thousand of'em pressed for about five hundred."

"Yeah, I might jump on that. Just let me think about it."

"Aight bet. Yo, let's go get somethin' ta eat." Shakim said grabbing the finished CD and handing it to Solo.

"That's you. But I'm a be real wit you. You make moves wit out me. Remember this shit ain't free."

"Man, I know that. I can't believe you even came at me like that. I'm ya brotha, not no Gimme man."

"I'm just makin sure. So down da road you don't be like I never told you."

"I'll tell you what," he said handing him back the CD and pullin out five hundred dollars. "You get wit ya people. Get that shit pressed and we'll split it, sixty forty. Now I'm hungry let's go eat." He said walking out the door.

Shakim realized that his business mind had interfered with his blood ties. He knew that the last thing Solo needed was any type of pressure on him. So he decided that for the rest of his stay he was gonna show him a good time. And that's what he did. First taking him to the various clubs, then to Shakim's favorite the strip joint. But that didn't turn out too good. While in V.I.P. one night, Solo started drinking a bunch of exotic drinks. Thai ice teas, blue motorcycles, green dinosaurs and such. That mixed with the hydro weed had him unconscious to everything going on around him. He didn't give any acknowledgement to the stars he ran into, he probably wouldn't have cared even if he were sober.

What killed everything was when they got back to Shakim's house. Solo was laying butt naked across the guest bed, when some of the night had wore off of him. He noticed that the sun wasn't up yet and looked at his watch, which read 4 o'clock in the morning. He couldn't have been here too long cause when he looked down he saw two females serving him. This made him sit up quick. "Yo, what da fuck ya'll doin'?"

"Your brother said to take care of you," one of the females, who was of oriental decent, said.

"Yeah and it's been about an hour. I thought you'd never come to," the other girl, who was a deep tanned white girl.

That there alone made him get up, because he didn't do the white girl thing even if it was just some head. "Get da fuck off me yo," he said jumping up. He wasn't so sober that he was ready to jump up and run around.

So he stumbled a bit as he look for his boxer's. When he found them he pounded out of the guest room and headed straight for his brother's room.

"Yo, Sha," he shouted as he went through the bedroom door. Shakim was in the middle of his own ménage' trios.

"What's up bruh?"

"Man, what da hell is goin' on?"

"What, you don't like ol' girl and them?"

"Man, I don't fuck wit no snow bunny man."

"My bust I ain't know. What you wanna switch?"

"Hell nah. I don't want none of 'em."

"Aight, if you say so. Send 'em in here."

Solo shook his head and went back to his room. He told them to get out and watched as they left. Seeing the erotic look in the Oriental's eyes as she waved by, he grabbed her arm. "You stay, you go," he said to the white girl pushing her out the room and slamming the door behind her. It wouldn't hurt to get a little Atlanta pussy. Diamond wouldn't like it, but she'd understand. As much as he hated to, he did make sure to use a rubber.

"Life is crazy ain't it?" Solo asked his brother as he set up the chessboard.

"You gotta ask yaself what is life."

"Life is livin."

"But what are you livin' for?" Shakim asked making his opening move.

"You know what? I never sat down to think of that."

"Why not?"

"Too busy runnin da streets. Chasin these girls. Getting money. Don't get me wrong, I got plans. Everybody think cause of who I be that all you gonna get is a bunch of violence. But since I been out there ain't been none of that goin on."

"Yeah, you got power, but what you gonna do wit it? Check."

"I'm tryin' ta give it back man. I want people to know that they can feel comfortable livin' in a community full of Sangres."

"And how you gonna do that? Check."

"About a month ago, I made an announcement that I wanted to start up an after school program."

"Wantin ta do somethin and doin' it is totally different. Your intentions are good, but it doesn't change nothin.

See me I'm doin what I love, music. So when you see me wit two, three women, I'm soakin up my success."

"You don't ever get bored? Wishin you had that special one in ya life? Check."
"Yeah, but when she comes, I don't know. I want her, but I ain't goin out my way to look for her."

"It's funny, how mine was right under my nose and I payed it no mind."

"So you sayin you committed now?" Shakim asked laughing.

"I can't say it's that, but I don't doubt if it'll end that way."

"Cause I was gonna say, da way you and Stacy were goin' at da other night had them other girls mad as hell."

"Yo, I ain't never had no Asian chick, so I had to try her."

"So what you gonna do?"

"I need to make a few calls. I told this cat I was gonna make plans ta build 1 rehab."

"So you givin' that part of ya life up huh? Mate."

"Damn! Let's play another one," Solo said setting the pieces back up. "Nah, not yet, but I'm a help rid some of da buyers out there, hopefully."

"Man you play chess like you live ya life. Ya strategy is good, but you quick ta put those closest to you in a bad predicament. But all I ca tell you is follow in da direction that you feel most comfortable wit."

"Word, I feel you."

"Everybody else is doin them, and you gotta think now it's your turn to do you."

With that in mind, Solo leaned back over the chessboard and made his opening move.

PART II - THE OPENING MOVE

CHAPTER 18

Solo was happier than he thought when he saw Diamond pull up at the airport. He jumped in da maroon Mazda 626 and gave her a kiss. "Miss me?"

"Me and everybody else."

"Why, what happened?"

"Nothing' really. You know how niggas is. They don't know how ta act when you take their leash off," she said pulling off.

"Dem my dogs."

"Yeah, in every way possible. So how was ya trip?"

"It was aight. Partied and bullshitted around."

"Fucked a few broads," she said eyeing him.

"See why you wanna go there."

"I'm sayin' cause I know you. And you ain't turnin' down no pussy. Not some new pussy anyway."

"How you know that?"

"So you sayin' you didn't?"

"Look…"

"Just what I thought. But I ain't sweatin it."

"What, you mad now?"

"Just as long as I don't see it or hear about it, cause if I do I'm a kill ya ass."

"Damn. For real?"

"Nah, but just don't do it no more aight. Cause you mine now and I ain't givin' that up for no hoe."

"Where we goin' now?"

"Ta your house and that's only ta help you pack."

"What you mean by that?" he asked smiling.

"I guess I shoulda asked huh?"

"What you want me ta move in wit you or something?"

"MmmHmm. Them three months you were gone seemed longer than those five years. I don't feel right when you away." Solo thought for a second. It was soon, but he had probably stayed at her crib more than anybody's, even his own, since he met her. Nah it wouldn't hurt to wake up next to somebody he could trust.

"Why your place?"

"Cause, yours is right in da middle of da Dust Bowl and I ain't tryin to be around that shit twenty-four hours a day.

"Aight, since it's your idea you pack, I ain't touchin shit."

"Oh you helpin'"

When Solo told her he wasn't gonna do nothing she thought he was joking. After watching her move around helplessly he still didn't move from his position, which was on the couch laid back. What he did do though was call up Kase and Chaos and told them to bring a small u-haul for his furniture. Diamond had a basement at her house, where he could put all his stuff. He already thought about how he was gonna turn it into his own private spot. The bedroom stuff will go into the extra one she had.

She owned a three-bedroom house on the outskirts of the city away from all the noise. Solo figured that the streets were treating her real well, cause the salary of a nurse wasn't that good. He knew that she managed a group of girls who stripped and ran an escort service. As long as none of them were Sangre he didn't care.

Still, living out as far as she did never appealed to him. He liked the inner city life, being around all the action. It kept you on point. Out there you liable to get comfortable and slip up. But he didn't mind. Like chess, some sacrifices had to be made for the better and what he was planning he needed somewhere safe to rest his head.

After everything was rearranged and set up Solo didn't stick around. He got Chaos to drop him off on Booker Street at his dope house. He knew that the spot was probably hot by now and should move it, but he had just got back and was only thinking about collecting. It had been two weeks and they were short on his doe, so he smacked them around a little bit and told them to tighten it up. He left and made his way over to Hue's house.

"Mind if I sit down?"

"Oh, you wanna mingle wit us peasants again?"

"It ain't even like dat," Solo said sitting beside Hue. He pulled out Precious and put it on his lap.

"You don't go nowhere wit out dat pistol do you?"

"Can't. Niggas wanna see me dead."

"Kill us then kill yaselves while ya'll at it, is that how it is?" Hue asked shaking his head.

"Nah, I told you what I'm tryin' ta do."

"When is this suppose ta happen? Cause I haven't even seen you around, let alone some rehab."

"I've been goin through some things. My grandma passed about three weeks ago."

"Oh, I ain't know. I'm sorry ta hear that."

"That's aight. I'm still tryin ta get over it myself. But I know one thing. When I do get that rehab goin, you better be first in line."

Hue chuckled, "Yeah, I'll be there, where ever there is."

"I might buy that land across da street tear dem houses down and put a center right there. Then buy that old store down da way. It's gonna take some work to rebuild that up. Give you some work ol man."

"It sounds good. They say seein is believin."

"You see how I took over da streets like before."

"That's what I be talkin about. It's easy ta take da streets cause that's all they gonna let you have. But once you switch over, you'll start seein vultures and snakes easin out of every crack and crevice. Then you ask yaself what you gonna do?"

Solo didn't say nothing because he knew Hue was telling the truth. All he knew was the streets, where he could solve any problem with his Precious. Yeah, it was easier to shoot a nigga and serve these fiends running around like zombies.

But after doing two bids he couldn't ignore his conscience that was eating at him to make a change. He didn't know if he could let it go. Nah, he knew that he couldn't. He had built up a strong family that could match any other set under his nation's umbrella. He couldn't stop what happened in the streets, all he could do was try to control it. It wasn't up to his people once he had the centers going. It was going to be up to those who needed help to go get it, because he was sure enough going to provide it. "I'll worry about that when it comes," he said answering Hue's question.

"Like I said, 'we see.' I hope you can change these streets around like they were when I first cam here."

"Solo!" someone hollered.

He looked around and didn't see anybody coming his way. Then a metallic gray Jeep Cherokee sped up to the front of Hue's crib and screeched to a stop. He quickly grabbed Precious and started to unload when he noticed that it was only Diamond.

"Yeah, I sure hop you can change 'em," Hue said.

"I don't know about how they were when you got here, but they'll change," Solo said stepping off the porch.

"Girl what da fuck wrong wit you rollin up like that. I was about ta shoot da shit out ya ass."

"Nigga, if I would've been anybody else, you would've been shot. Get in."
"For what?"

"I gotta show you somethin'."

"This better be important," he said go around to the passenger side. "I just got back and you already buggin," he mumbled as he got in the jeep.

"I bet you won't be sayin' that when you see this." Solo just looked at her. Then he caught the glint of something between her feet. "Whose car is this?"

"Qiana's."

"Is that Qiana's too?" he asked pointing at her feet. Diamond followed the direction his finger was pointing at and seen he was talking about the gun she had went and got before picking him up. "Nah, that's mine." She answered focusing back on the road.

Solo reached down and pulled the gun from its hiding spot. He recognized it immediately as the same gun he had used in the war with the Congrejoes. "I was wonderin what happened to this joker," he said turning the Heckler Koch Mp SK 9m submachine gun back and forth in his hand.

"You left it wit me remember?"

"I told you ta get rid of it for me too," he said eyeing her.

"That things like a trophy now, I couldn't get rid of it after helpin you like it did." She was talking about the gun like it was some type of archangel.

"You right about that, but it's still hot and I don't want it around me."

Diamond let out a deep sigh. "Alright, I'll get rid of it as soon as we finish handling this."

"Handlin' what? And where da fuck we goin '?" he asked watching the trees get thicker as they passed the Mcleansville prison.

"I rather you see it for yourself than me tell you."

"Who da hell would stay way out here ta see somethin' goin' on?"

"Qiana would."

Solo didn't say no more. He knew that with the second mention of Qiana that it was something serious, because Qiana didn't or wouldn't call no body for no bullshit. When they pulled up to Qiana's house, they got out and Qiana opened the door like she'd been waiting on them impatiently to return. Solo hugged and kissed her as he walked in teasing her.

"Yo what's really goin' on, huh?"

"Just chill and watch," Diamond said.

"Watch what?" he didn't know what was going one. Qiana took him to the back door and pointed at a house that was on a hill. He saw the house but if there was supposed to be anything else he was lost.

"They ain't come out yet."

"Who?"

"You'll see. These mothafucka couldn't have been here no more than three, four months, cause that's when I went out of town. About two three days ago I was puttin some clothes out to dry and I noticed people comin' and goin'. I'm thinkin' it's just some new neighbors, but too much traffic was goin' on to be way out here. So I had ta be nosy. You know how that go can't trust nobody. So I go gets some binoculars and start watchin' and what I saw had me mad as hell."

"What was that?"

"That house right there is full of Congrejoes, but that ain't da thing. I wasn't tryin' ta jump da gun, so I played my position. It wasn't until what I saw today that made me call Diamond up."

"Quit edgin' me on and tell me what da fuck you saw."

"Like I said it's better that you see it ya self," Diamond said.

"Go get me your binoculars then Qi," he said ready to see what the big deal was besides a bunch of Congrejoes.

He didn't get to see nothing though until night fell and that was only after Qiana got his attention.

"There they go look," she said pointing at the house. Solo put the binoculars to his eyes and the first thing he noticed was the Silver Diamante. He figured that it could've been anybody's, and then he saw her. Kenya was coming out hugged up on some dude. He couldn't see who cause she blocked his face, but she looked real happy. "I knew that bitch was fuckin' somebody," he mumbled. Then he watched as she leaned in to kiss the guy and when she pulled back, he shot out of the chair he was sitting in. "Ain't this a bitch." He said to himself feeling the anger radiate through his body. "Yeah I got your ass now." You would think that he couldn't get any madder than he was. But when he saw Kenya pull back her coat and let the dude rub on her stomach, he proved you wrong. "I'm a kill that motherfucker." Who he was talking about was his childhood friend Diavante.

When he turned around his face was so red you'd think that the devil had switched bodies with him. "Qiana, I want you to get rid of that bitch."

"My pleasure," Qiana said running into the back room to change clothes. "Diamond her friends...."

"Baby, I'm already on it I was just waiting on the da green light."

"I'm through waitin'. This shit starts now" he said walking out the front door.

He went to Diamond's car that was parked in front of the house. "Diamond let's go!" he hollered still feeling the heat boiling inside.

When they pulled off, Solo snatched up Diamond's phone that was plugged into the cigarette lighter and dialed Pinero's number. "Go by the house." "Yo. P get everybody together KC and Cross and come to Diamond's crib...and in a hurry. Don't hesitate, shit's bout to get real ugly in da "Boro." The way Solo was pacing back and forth in front of his top dogs, he could've burnt a path in the carpet. They were sitting in Diamond's living room watching Solo walk the length of the living room. The smoking Newport in his hand, reminded them of the many Tupac scenes they had seen. If they didn't know any better they would've thought he had taken a few sniffs of powder.

"Look, ya'll know I ain't got ya'll out here for nothin'. And you knew shit was gonna jump off before long. All I wanna know is is ya'll ready for what's 'bout to happen?" he asked looking at each one of them, but not stopping his pace.

"That's all me and Kase been waitin' on, for you ta give us da word," Chaos said.

"What about you?"

"You know I rolls wit you."

Solo looked at Diamond. "That shouldn't even be a question."

"O.G. Cross? If you ain't ready let me know."

"I wasn't there for da last war, and I ain't tryin' ta miss this one. Plus, I got a gun supply."

"What kind of gun supply?"

"Any kind you want I got. AR-15s, sks' Aks, Krugers, Glocks, Inf beams, whatever you need."

Solo looked at Diamond thinking that she knew about this and forgot to tell him, but she just shrugged her shoulders.

Cross saw the silent moves and smiled. "Man, I ain't no dummy. I knew this was gonna happen sooner or later, so I've been stockin' and sellin' 'em on da low.

Solo looked at Cross, who could've passed for his younger brother, if not his son. That's how much he resembled him in looks and thinking. He just smiled, "My boy," Aight this what we gonna do…" Solo explained everything. Taking the rests opinions and input as he went along until everything was established. This game could no longer be stalled as the board was set up and the pieces put in their position. When they left Diamond's house he had already pushed his pawn up.

CHAPTER 19

Silk had been in the game for a minute. He had gained enough money with his little click, he was about ready to retire. The only thing he couldn't stop being was a Congrejo. But he did what an O-G. was supposed to do. Stay on the low and clean. Keep unnecessary heat off of you. So he wondered why he was being pulled over by an undercover cop at that. He stared at the red flashing light in his rearview as the undercover got out of his car.

"May I see your license and registration please?"

"What seems to be the problem officer?" Silk asked looking at the clean-cut brown skinned officer at his window as he reached in the glove compartment for his registration.

"Nothing really, we just been lookin for a suspect that was drivin' in a car that's similar to yours."

"I can assure you that it isn't me," he said handing him the requested items.

"Is that so" the officer said looking at Silk's license then handing it back. "I guess you're right. You're just another victim of D.W.C."

Silk started to agree, but didn't know what the C stood for. "What da hell is D.W.C.?"

"Drivin' while Congrejo" with that the officer pulled out his automatic P90 and unloaded on Silk. Then acting like nothing happened, he walked back to his car and pulled off.

Chaos hadn't tortured somebody in so long he was acting all giddy. Driving down a dirt road headed into the country, he was followed by Kase and two of their soldiers. Each one had a Congrejo in the SUV's they were driving and the one in Chaos' car was getting on his nerves. "Shut up nig."

"Man, I ain't do nothin'"

"Don't get scared now. This is what it's all about. Ta live 'n' die for yours."

"Man, come on man. You can have that block man, just don't kill me, man."

"Didn't I say shut up?"

When they got to where they were going Chaos jumped out the car and went to the back of it. The way Kase and Chaos snatched the struggling bodies out onto the dirt clearing, you would've thought that they were rag dolls. But this is what they were used to doing, snatching people up with ease.

"Who's first?" Chaos asked looking down at the four people on the ground. "It don't matter, they all goin'," Charles answered. He finally got moved up to second string and was running his own spot.

"So pick somebody then," Chaos barked at him.

Charles grabbed the guy he wanted to get rid of personally. Kase pulled out some chains and had everybody turn their cars around. He tied a limb to the back of each suv that had the guy spread eagled. When they all got into a vehicle and pulled off, all you could hear was the screams as the guy's limbs were ripped out of their sockets. This is why Chaos had the name he went by, because he caused total Chaos wherever he went.

"Okay, who's next?" Chaos said jumping out of the Montero sport.

"Do you know who I am?" Cross asked the guy who was hanging from the ceiling in the position of a person being crucified. He was sitting in a metal folding chair with a blunt in his hand.

"Yeah, I know who you are. What ya'll Sangres set trippin' now?"

"Set trippin'? Nah, we wouldn't do a thing like that. See this is just some unfinished business from a while. Say, five years ago."

"Ho! That petty ass war, man that was nothin'"

"You right. It's nothing' cause I wasn't in it. But see I don't know how you feel about your superior, but mine is like a father to me. So when he asks me to do somethin'. I don't hesitate."

"And you think my soldiers gonna let you get away this? If so, you got da game fucked up."

"Da thing about me is, I expect everything, but if you separate da head from da body, da body loses its direction." Cross got up and walked towards the hanging figure. "Do you believe in god?" ... Huh? As you can see I have a thing for crosses," he said lifting up one of the medallions resting on his chest. "But that's not why they all me Cross. Well maybe a little bit."

"Do what you gotta do you little punk. I always wanted ta know if there was a hell." "Not so fast," Cross said, picking up a sharp pointed pipe. "They say when they pierced Jesus' side out flowed blood and water, but you are not Jesus, so all I should see is blood," he said shoving the pipe under his ribs and watched as the blood poured down the body and onto the floor.

When he thought a good amount of blood had left out of the body, he got one of his boys to pour kerosene and gasoline mixed down the guy's throat. At least two gallons were forced down into the guy's body before the liquid was ignited. "See you in hell," Cross said raising his blunt, then taking a puff, as he watched the body burn from the inside out.

As soon as Solo and Diamond had left, Qiana wasn't too far behind. Dressed in all black fatigues, she looked like a midnight burglar. Her dark complexion only helped her out.

She grabbed her knife and Beretta, every girl's favorite gun, then headed out the door. She had to time it right in order to let Kenya get in front of her. This is what she lived for, that gangsta shit. So it wasn't a thing to get rid of someone for her people. Plus, she never liked Kenya no more than Diamond did. And truth be told, if it wasn't for Diamond, she would've been pushed up on Solo, so out of respect she fell back and got up with his man Pinero. If she couldn't have the best, she'd settle for the next in line. She was feeling P too. Even more so when they went to Virginia Beach for those few months after that murder. Only thing she didn't like was how his cell phone stayed going off. She was glad that he didn't stay with her because he'd have to get a new phone. She wasn't gonna have all that interruption goin gon, especially if they were in the middle of something.

'Damn, where the fuck this girl stay at', Qiana thought to herself as she kept following Kenya. After awhile, she figured that ol' girl wasn't going straight home. She looked at the clock on the dashboard. 9:30. Well it is kinda early she thought. Of course everybody had ta go to work in the morning, but that didn't mean that this couldn't get done tonight. She knew from past experience that when Solo wanted to set something off he didn't care what time or day it was, it was going down.

Him and Diamond probably will wait till tomorrow to get the people they wanted, because Diamond told her how she was gonna set Kenya's little clit up and it could only be done right during business hours. But for the rest of them, she knew that by the time the sun rose, some bodies were gonna pop up missing.

Qiana had stopped following Kenya around after she made one too many stops. So she called Diamond and them and found out her address, then went and waited for her to come home.

When Kenya walked into her apartment, she felt exhausted. After talking to David, she realized how weak he was compared to Solo. That's why she had taken things into her own hands. Thinking that she could have the best of both worlds, she went after Solo. That was her mistake; still she knew he wouldn't do anything as long as she stayed out of his sight. Oh, she still wanted to get him and Pinero, but that was in due time.

She was close to seven months pregnant and didn't need to be on her feet like she was. She was mad that Solo didn't think the baby was his, and even madder that David said it was his. On one of her check ups she had a sonogram taken and found out she was having a boy. 'Fuck him,' she thought. He'll believe it's his after he takes that blood test. She was so tired all she wanted to do was take a bath and go to sleep. She went into the bathroom and ran some bath water at the same time stripping out of her clothes and putting them in her hamper.

Naked, except for a robe to cover her, she walked into her bedroom while waiting for the tub to fill up. She didn't notice the dark figure sitting in the corner when she cut the light on.

"Man, I thought you'd never come home," Qiana said sitting up in the arm chair. Kenya gave a frightening jump and gasped. "What are you doing in my house?"

"Some ol' friends wanted me to check up on ya. Make sure everything was alright," she said getting out of the chair and moving towards Kenya.
"What ol' friends?"

"Who do you think? Surely not ya boy David."

Automatically she knew who sent this girl standing in front of her. She tried to run but was stopped in midstep, when Qiana grabbed a handful of her hair. "Not so fast. Stick around for a while."

Kenya tried to fight her but was quickly dazed by the butt of a gun. Qiana pulled her onto her bed and tied her arms and legs to the bed posts.

"Solo ain't have enough heart to do this himself?"

"Ha! Oh, he got da heart; he just ain't wanna touch you. And you don't know how long we've been waitin' to do this. See you fucked up."

"I'm havening his baby, doesn't he care about that?

"Nope. Once he saw you wit ya little buddy today, all hope for you was thrown out da window and I've been given da honor to make sure of it. And this baby thing, we'll take care of that right now," she said pulling out a hawk blade. "Nooooooo," Kenya screamed as she tried to break the rope binding her to the bed.

"Yeeaah,"

Qiana replied shoving the blade into Kenya's abdomen and slit a hole big enough to stick her hand in. It happened so fast that Kenya witnessed all the pain and even saw the baby being pulled out of her before losing unconsciousness. She was then untied and placed in her tub with the dead baby laying across her chest. To make sure she was dead as well, Qiana slit her throat.

When she walked out of the apartment, she stripped out of her outer garments and walked to where she was parked, grabbing a trash bag she brought with her, she put everything into it. Toboggan, gloves, shoes, socks, pants and sweatshirt, then tied the bag. She drove to a rural spot and burned the bag. After watching the last of the evidence she went home.

Pinero was never the one to torture people. He felt it was a waste of time. Yeah, it served its purpose but it wasn't him. He was a gun clapper and everybody under him was a gun clapper. He played it like it was supposed to be, a war. Grabbing two of his lieutenants, he rolled up on every Congrejo spot he knew and murdered everybody in the house, sparing no one.

It didn't matter, if you were a mother, father, cousin, aunt, uncle, sister, brother, nephew or niece. You weren't gonna be alive when they left.

Yeah, this was the start of something big. All grudges were about to be settled. Bottled up hate was gonna be released. This was worse than any terrorist attack, because the whole city was in danger. When you had two strong forces going head on all that would be left is chaos.

The sad part was that those on the receiving end didn't know what it was over and probably never will. The Sangres didn't care if you knew or not, right now it was about surviving. Either you did or died trying.

CHAPTER 20

Diamond stood in the clothing store across the street from the bank Porsha worked in. They had transferred their money to another bank after Solo left Kenya to make sure nothing "Accidentally" happened. She could see through the glass window as the delivery guy handed Porsha her message. She signed for it then began to read it. When Diamond saw her shaking her head and smiling, she left the store and called Charlotte.

"Girl, I don't know what Kenya up to. All I know is she left a message saying to meet her at the Radisson, there'll be a key waiting," Porsha said talking to Torri and Jocelyn.

"Why ain't you call her ask?" Torri asked, not feeling this secretive stuff.

"Cause she said don't. But you know Kenya. She always trying to pull some slick shirt. Probably got some niggas she trying to gaffle."

"Now that I'd understand." Jocelyn threw in.

"It better be, 'cause my baby was supposed to come get me today."

"Torri, everybody's your baby. As long as they got a big dick and some cash you swear you in love."

"Hey, ain't that what we about? The Money Hungry Clit. Don't forget it girl."

"I know that's right," Jocelyn and Porsha said together.

They rode up in silence in the elevator to the top floor where they had a key to a suite. When they got to the room Porsha unlocked the door and walked in. "Kenya, we here," she hollered out.

"At least there's some food," Torri said seeing some dishes on a table.

Jocelyn turned to close the door, but it was done for her as she looked into the eyes of Charlotte. "Who the fuck are you?"

"I'm just the girl next door, come to pay my respects."

"Thank you, but no thank you. You can go on back next door."

"Nah, not before my girls introduce themselves."

"Your girls, what girls?" Porsha asked, but her question was soon answered as Karen and Qiana walked out of the bedroom. "What the fuck is going on? What is this about?"

"That's a good question," Diamond said as she came out of the bathroom drying her hands on a towel.

"I knew this shit wasn't right," Torri said angrily.

"Shut up Torri. Diamond what is this all about."

"Ya girl Kenya. She crossed my family, our family. And more importantly my heart."

"I told her not to do it "Fuck"

"I guess you were sayin' da wrong words."

"What is she talking about Porsha?" Jocelyn demanded.

"Solo. She was fuckin' wit Solo, who's a Sangre, while messin' wit David..."

"A Congrejo," Jocelyn finished for her.

"So, now that that's out da way. They always told me, what's good for da goose is good for da gander. Ain't that right Qiana?"

"Yup," she answered and before they knew what to do, they each had a piano string wrapped around their neck, sucking the life out of them.

They fought and struggled, but when you a corporate person going against street people, you don't stand a chance. The only person who was any trouble was Torri, but that didn't last long either when Diamond knocked the wind out of her.

"That's a feisty one there. Too bad, she could a probably been some good on our team. "Put 'em around da table, like they were about to eat," Diamond commanded. They sat them around the coffee table. Two on a couch the other on the love seat. They looked like they had fallen asleep the way they were slumped on the sofas.

After wiping everything down they walked out the room and put a do not disturb sign on the doorknob. Diamond wasn't worried about them looking for her, because the room was in the name of a Kenya Jones, who was right now deceased.

Everything was going the way Solo wanted it to. Instead of going from bottom to top, he told them to start from the top and work their way down. He didn't know what or how David kept such a weak tem together, because too many high ranked people were slipping. Not like he cared, but he thought he'd have some trouble. Sitting at home, he thought his plan out. If he survived this, he was gonna step back and let someone else run his set. What he was gonna focus on was building some businesses for his people, to get them off the street. That's if he survived, but he didn't expect to survive. Because this time there wasn't a thing going to stop him from redeeming his brother's death. He looked at the weapons scattered on the basement floor with an observant eye. He wanted to make sure that he had something for any situation that came his way.

He shook his head thinking where did Cross get all this artillery and what was he gonna do with what he didn't need. He stopped when he heard someone moving upstairs. "D, is dat you?" he asked grabbing one of the choppers he was going to use.

"Yeah, it's me."

Solo satisfied that it was his girl put the guns back in the trunk they came in. He put the ones he was gonna keeping a black duffel bag. Grabbing everything he needed and headed upstairs.

Seeing that it was still early, he put the bag against the wall and went into the back room where he and Diamond kept their computers. Since he didn't have a newspaper he looked it up on the Internet. He wanted to know if anything was said about what was going on. He couldn't find nothing but knew it wouldn't be long before something was brought, even if it was a little snippet, which he knew better than. These scenarios were gonna be front page. Just as he was cutting the computer off, he saw Diamond walk pass his vision drying her hair off. He got up to follow her in their room and seen that all she had covering her was a robe, that was slightly parted. Of course since he'd been with her, he's seen her naked plenty of times, but he still liked to look at her.

Walking up behind her while she was brushing her hair in the mirror, he kissed her on her neck. Then ran his hand down the front of her body and noticed that her flat stomach wasn't as flat as it usually was. "What's this?" he asked rubbing her stomach. "To many Heinekens?" he joked.

"You know I don't drink," she pointed out catching his eyes in the mirror, and then raised an eyebrow as if to say,

"You should know what it is."

"How long?" he asked already knowing that she was pregnant, by the way she acted when she thought he wasn't looking. He just didn't know why she hadn't told him, but he already knew the answer to that as well.

"I found out a week after you went out of town. And before you go off askin' 'why I ain't told you', think about when I had da chance? I see this was da only way ta get 'cha attention," she said turning around letting the robe open up.

"Damn, you act like I was gonna punch you in ya head or somethin'. I seen you havin' mornin' sickness, so I already knew. But you could've told me when you picked me up from da airport."

"You right. I should've but..."

"Don't worry 'bout it," he said cutting her off. "But you know you gotta stay home now. I can't take da chance of somethin' happenin' to you and my baby."

"But..."

"No buts, after I get rid of this nigga, then we sit and talk about us," he said bending to kiss her before he walked out the room.

When he got to the middle of the living room he skipped and realized that he might not ever set eyes on Diamond again. Turning around he went back in the bedroom and seen Diamond was still standing how he left her.

Grabbing her face in his hands he looked into her eyes for what might be the last time. "You know I love you right. I want you to know that before I walk out da door."

"I love you too, Solo. I always have, since da first night I've met," she said trying to hold back her tears, but couldn't. Solo bent to kiss her with his whole heart, then turned to leave for the last time. Diamond opened her mouth to say something, as she watched Solo leave, but held it in. How bad she wanted to go with him, to make sure he had someone to watch his back. She knew exactly where he was headed. She didn't want to get him mad if he found out she was following him. But she didn't want to take any chances of losing him to a 'what if.' Quickly getting dressed, she ran downstairs to the basement to get a few guns of her own.

One thing David didn't need was a newspaper clipping telling him what was going on. He was witnessing it first-hand. He should've done something as soon as Pinero shot Splash. Without him, it opened hip up a little bit. And like a wedged door, all you needed was a crack to get in. He knew it wasn't going to be long before a war jumped off again. He never believed that bullshit he told Splash, because he knew Solo, and Solo never forgave nor forgot. He knew he couldn't sit there wasting time, he had to be the leader he worked so hard for. 'So this was how it was gonna be,' he thought to himself. 'Well I'm ready Mr. Solomon Divine....'

CHAPTER 21

Solo could care less what was going on in the city, his mind was focused on what was sitting out pass the city limits. He was driving an old pitch black Chevy Blazer, with Pinero riding shotgun. Pinero had left his soldiers with instructions not to stop till he told them to. He wasn't gonna miss any situation to ride out with his best friend and superior.

"Yo, I don't care who out here, everybody's dyin' tonight," Pinero voiced.

"Do you, just save me dat nigga David."

When they got to the spot where they needed to be they pulled in Qiana's back yard and cut the engine.

"Go and tell Qiana and dem we out here waitin'." Pinero disappeared around the truck and five minutes later came back with six people. Four guys and two girls. He passed out a few of the guns in the duffel bag, then told them what he wanted.

After everyone understood what to do they crept up the hill to the secluded house. Diamond sat in the shadows watching.

It didn't take long before bullets began flying. Two Congrejoes were sitting on the porch running their mouth when they got hit. It was too late to take heed to David's warnings. Even though they had the upper when they snuck up on the house, it wasn't that easy once they got inside. David knew Solo was coming so he waited for him. He knew Solo knew where he lived, just like he knew one of his Sangres bitches lived down the hill. He had moved in this house for a reason, to prepare for what he knew eventually was gonna come. What he didn't expect was it to be in the middle of the winter.

When he heard the first shots outside, he tensed up and felt his palms become sweaty. But that soon died down as he picked up a chopper of his own and headed to the stairs with two of his boys in front of him. The first two people who caught their bullet, before his boys did, were the two girls. He fell back to protect himself from the aimless shots headed in his direction.

Solo had come the back way with two of his boys. He saw Tabitha and Karen hit the floor when a bullet pierced through their torsos. There were doors opening everywhere as Congrejoes flooded the house. He realized the trap he ran into, but he came with one thing on his mind and wasn't gonna let nothing stop him till it was done. He reached into his pocket and grabbed the round piece of metal that he had put there earlier.

He tried not to laugh in such a serious situation, but he thought about the Scarface movie and chuckled "Ya'll get back," he yelled to his people before tossing the grenade into the crowd.

He didn't know why Cross had it or why he picked it up, but he was glad about both as the loud explosion helped even out the odds. The media might label this more than a gang war. More like a Greensboro Massacre.

This probably what it was like in 'Nam' Solo thought as the M-80 exploded in his hands with each pull of the trigger leaving whoever it hit unable to stay amongst the living. He wished this was a one-sided fight, but when he was reloading his gun and didn't hear any more shots being fired, he realized the only people standing was him and Pinero. He looked around and even though there was a large quantity of Congrejoes sent to the afterlife, he had lost eight of his own.

Qiana must've sent two more after the girls got shot. One of those two happened to be Charles. He knew that by the time this was over that there was going to be a lot of funerals and wakes, let alone hospital bills. Maybe even his own. But this wasn't the right time to dwell on such a thing. This game was far from over and he was out to win not stale mate.

Listening he heard some movement upstairs and knew it had to be David. The icy cold air that was blowing through the front and back doors would've made the average man shiver. But when you had pints of adrenaline pumping through your veins you felt anything but average.

The only way they knew how to get up the stairs without getting shot down was to press their backs against the wall and waste a few bullets as they went up. And this is exactly what they did.

When they got to the top of the stairs they could see David trying to open a window. Pinero quickly worked his long limbs and snatched David back before he could leap out the window.

"Where you going', my nigga, huh?" Solo asked smacking him in the face with the butt of his gun.

"Man do what you gotta do, quit stallin', 'less you scared," David looked up at Solo through his eyes, which started to bruise where he hit him.

Solo got face to face with him. "Naww, Diavante', you know I ain't scared. I've been waiting almost fifteen years for this and I ain't gonna fuck it up. Just one question. Why you'd do it? You could've came wit me. We could've had it all man. And of all people, you had to kill da one you know I cared for da most."

"That's da whole point. I didn't wanna be ya shadow no more. It was too much about you. I had to do me, earn my own name and status. And you see I did."

"You could a still earned a name and had stats like me, but you didn't want it."

"Like you, I didn't wanna be like you. That's why I did what I did."

"And wit dat, ya fate was sealed. You of all people should know, you don't dare cross da Divines."

"Fuck you and da Divines."

"And you just fucked ya self." He said pulling Precious out his shoulder holster but was stopped when a closet door busted open.

"It seems like we have some unfinished business," Splash said standing in da doorway with two .40 magnums pointed at Pinero and Solo. They were frozen in shock, all except David who was grinning from ear to ear.

"How da fu..." Pinero mumbled in disbelief.

"It's called bullet proof. Those talons penetrated but not deep enough."

Pinero knew he was in a no win situation, but he rather die fighting than to just die. The last thing he got to do was lift the chopper in his hand before four bullets pierced his body, two in the chest, one in the stomach and the other in the head. He wasn't as lucky as Splash, nor did he have time to let off a shot.

Solo watched as his right hand man and best friend dropped to the floor dead. He knew it but didn't want to believe it.

"You don't seem too confidant now do you," Diavante' said getting off the floor. "Splash handle this for me so we can attend o some better business.

"My pleasure," Splash said stepping forward and raising his guns. Solo knew not to raise his gun, because it would on draw his death faster.

He wanted to live as long as possible, long enough to at least put a bullet in Diavante'. He saw Splash point the magnum at his face and started to raise his own gun.

"Noooooooo," Solo heard a voice say right before the all too familiar sound of his Mp capsized Splash in front of his face. Naw, there wouldn't be no coming back this time. He turned to see Diamond standing holding the machine gun by her side.

"Don't tell me you wish I stayed home," she said with a tight grin. Then nodded at the window. "He's getting away." Solo looked to see the window was all the way opened. He looked out and seen Diavante' heading to a car. Solo flew out the room and skipped half the stairs on his way down. You could hear the snow that had built up over the last two days, crunching under his black leather Timberland boots, as he ran to the Blazer. He was glad that he had this SUV in this weather, because of its four wheel drive he wouldn't run into any problems.

By now Diamante' had a head start on him, but this was a straight away, so it wouldn't be hard to catch up to him. By the time he did catch up to him, he was in the city limits and Solo wondered where the hell he thinks he was headed. There wasn't a side of town that wasn't part of this war. He was right on his bumper when he turned on Market Street. Ten again as he turned left on Greene Street. 'He's headin' to da projects,'

Solo thought and felt that he had him. He patted his pockets for his phone and remembered that he left at home. 'Damn', beating the steering wheel. At the same time realizing that his intention wasn't just to go into the projects, but to pass the police station going ninety miles an hour.

If his plan was to get the attention of the Greensboro Police Department it worked. Solo felt at a loss, until he saw a phone on the passenger seat. It probably was Pinero's, he thought picking it up and dialing as fast as his fingers could.

"Yo, who dis," Cross spoke into the phone.

"Solo where you at?"

"I'm headed to da Southside to help Kase –n-em. What's all dat in da background sound like bubbletop?"

"It is, I'm headed dat way. I need a road block on Elm down by South Street."

"It's live out there man, they standin' like there in L.A."

"Well I'm bringn' bubble top to feel some of it too. And I'm a minute away."

"Aight I gotcha."

When Solo hung up he didn't think he was gonna get the block, even though it was actually three minutes instead of one. But when they had made down to South Street, you could see cars lined up blocking the way. And you could see Congrejoes and Sangres shooting it out.

They had driven right into the line of fire. But one thing they both knew, especially Solo, was that even though they were at war, when police come all guns ended up being pointed at them. This made them fall back, especially when Solo jumped out firing another chopper he pulled from the duffel bag in the back.

He had almost got lost in the shooting when he saw Diavante' out of the corner of his eye dash through the projects. Solo quickly took off after him. This time he had Precious cocked and ready as he ran passed each building.

Solo knew Diavante' wasn't long winded runner like him. So all he had to do was give chase till he was tired, which was in the middle of Smith Homes, Sangre territory. He didn't hesitate to let his girl finally release some tension. The bullet struck him in the back and sprawled him on the ground face first. He walked over to him and kicked him square in the mouth four or five times. "That's for my mother," he said the shot him in the leg the stepped on the wound. That's for my nigga, P," He used his foot to turn him over then pressed the boot on his throat. "Don't die yet nigga, don't die yet," he said squatting over him. He put the gun in his mouth and emptied the clip "For my brother."

Solo looked to da sky as a tear started form. "You can rest now T, I got him for you, I got him." He peered down into the unrecognizable face of Diavante' with a look of hate still in his eyes. He didn't feel anything as he walked off through the forming crowd of Sangres telling them not to touch the body. Let the dead bury their own.

He didn't think about all the mothers that will be crying and dressed in black in the next few days. It wasn't that he didn't care; it was just at this point in time his mind wasn't focused on it. He wouldn't realize what happened until he snapped out of what seemed to be a dream.

CHAPTER 22

His prediction was right. There was to be a lot of hospital bills and funeral arrangements. Plus, he knew it was going to take loner than a week for the remaining Congrejoes to realize the war was over as far as he was concerned. Even through he knew that by the way he killed their superior, it wouldn't truly be over. It only meant that what was before was no longer going to happen. No more intermingling or walking amongst each other loosely. Not like you could let your guard down before. It was just now, the tension would be so thick the wrong glance will send bullets flying.

Sections were going to be claimed serious this time around. It wouldn't hurt any of the Sangres, being that they had the inner city on lock. It would be bad on the Congrejoes, who could only claim the outskirts where the upper and middle class lived. It wasn't his concern where they went and didn't care. He had gotten rid of his problem and expected anyone else under him to do the same.

Solo sighed then looked over at Diamond. Her petite frame could no longer hide the bulge in her stomach that had five months of growth in it. As happy as he wanted to be this wasn't a time of joy. He looked down at his clothes. The same black suit he wore to his grandmother's funeral. In his lap was a trench coat concealing Precious.

He hoped that this was the last time he'd be wearing this suit. The only funeral he wanted to attend after this was his own.

Standing up, he made his way towards the casket to pay his respects. He saw that the mortician did a good job with covering up the bullet hole in his head even though he could see where it entered. Maybe because he knew where it entered at, being that he saw it firsthand. He also knew that if he lifted up his head only half of the back would be there. Not even the mortician was that good. The longer he stared at him, the more he seemed not to look like the person he befriended over thirteen years ago. It was sort of like his cousin down in South Carolina.

When he went to that funeral, no one agreed that he looked like the cousin or nephew Elijah, they all remembered. Pinero wasn't that bad though. But this was no longer Pinero, just an empty vessel. "It's been a long journey my boy. You fought wit da best of 'em. I'll neva forget 'cha. So I guess I'll see you when I see ya," he whispered to the corpse. Pulling a green flag out of his pocket, he placed it across his chest. "I love you, my nigga," he said before turning around.

Solo looked at all the different faces attending the wake. The room was mostly filled with Sangres. A close cousin, who was a Congrejo, tried to go unnoticed on the back wall. He nodded at Solo to let him know that him being there wasn't a threat. Solo gave a slight nod back. He continued to scan the room. Seeing a tight faced brother with his two daughters who didn't fully understand what was going on. He saw the misty eyes of aunts and baby mothers. It had totally slipped his mind that Pinero had kids. The two girls, even with different mothers still resembled their father.

Yeah, he'd have to help take care of them. They had promised each other that if one of them were to go, the other would take care of their seed like they were his own. And Solo never broke a promise.

Finally, Solo's eyes ended up locked with Kim, Pinero's mother. She knew almost everything about Solo. She felt that he was the realest friend Pinero had. In fact his whole family felt that way. She searched his eyes for some kind of answer as to what happened. All she knew was that he was shot four times. He didn't know what they told the police when they took him to the hospital. He couldn't lie to her, because she knew that anything her son got into, if he wasn't there with him or had his hand in it, he knew something about it. He couldn't deny it, because that's how it always was.

One didn't do anything without the other one being there or at least knowing about it. He couldn't deny it, because that's how it always was. But what do you say, what could you say to a grieving mother who just lost her youngest boy? As he looked into Kim's eyes, he could feel water forming in his own, but he held them back. He went and sat down after realizing there was nothing he could tell her to soothe her soul.

After about two to three hours of people taking turns to look at the lifeless body, that once held the soul of a man who only had the love of his family and Solo, they prepared to go to the graveyard.

As Solo stood near the freshly dug hole, that stopped at five feet instead of the normal six, he watched as the pallbearers carried Pinero's casket across the grassy hill.

People had thought that he would be one of the bears, but he didn't want to touch nothing resembling death. Because as much as he denied being superstitious, when it came to certain things, that's exactly what he was.

When the pastor began speaking and quoting verses, Solo's thought started to wonder. He had no interest in what was being said. He as well as Pinero followed an unorthodox form of Islam, but it was the family's wishes to let a man of the Church speak at the funeral. Shoot, he was better off speaking. This man didn't know P not one bit. It didn't matter if he was speaking kindly of him. He'd probably be laughing his ass off if he heard this guy talk.

Yeah, he was loving, but he only loved his fam. Three-fourth of these people wouldn't even get a glance from him let alone love. Even those he loved he fought, but that was part of the love. Everybody else he didn't waste energy on. Nah, he wasn't gonna go through all this. He was gonna get cremated.

Have them place him on a mantle, so they could think about him every time they walked by. He might give them nightmares. Ha! Now that would be something. Still he wanted no one to speak on or about him except someone who really knew him. Like his sister or wife.

Whoa! Wife? Now what made him think of that? At the same time he unconsciously looked over at Diamond, then at her round stomach. In the short time they were really together, he had learned more than all the years they knew each other. He finally realized he sincerely loved her after that night. How couldn't he? But wifey? He wasn't too sure of. Oh, she was more than the right type, but it was too soon.

And when he thought she wasn't paying any attention, she looked up at him, and put a soft smile on her face. Looking at this he knew that she'd be the one to make him out to be a liar.

As they started to lower the casket, the Sangres that were there stepped up and threw their green flags in behind it. Diamond followed suit by untying the bandana she had holding her hair back from her face and tossing it in the death hole.

Solo was glad that the funeral was over. He was ready to leave. While the other people headed to the reception to either get over the hump, try to forget, or just plain get some free food, Solo stood observing the area. He wasn't about to try and 'mingle with the folks' as they would say. He couldn't even begin to think of forgetting this soon. In fact he would never forget about Pinero. He had a permanent spot in his heart and mind that not even the Most High could take away from him.

He still had a grim look on his face when Diamond walked up next to him and stood there looking like the missing part of his life that she was. She was his other half, the better half. At time playing his conscience. And he happily accepted that because she wasn't on of those loud mouthy broads who thought they knew everything. She went along with whatever he decided to do, which was usually what she suggested anyway. That was only because she knew what was going on. She wasn't on the outside looking. She was right in the middle of it all whenever something went. If his gun blazed so did hers. If he punched someone, she'd kick them. They were better than any Bonnie and Clyde.

Solo put his arm around her shoulder and began walking off. He only took about ten steps before he stopped. "What's wrong?" Diamond asked looking up at Solo. "Something ain't right. It's too quiet. Niggas were still shootin' it out last night and everybody knew dat this funeral was jumpin' off today."

"Maybe they gave up or respect da dead." She said shrugging.

"You know like I know that dat's not it," Solo looked around more openly at the crossing street sections. He didn't know what it was but he could feel it. Maybe he was imagining it, but wasn't sure. After awhile he just shrugged his shoulders and started walking again. Just as he got ready to step off the curb and cross the street headed to his car, he saw them.

The white van that looked like a painting crew could've fooled anybody if they weren't expecting it. But that was the thing about Solo, he expected the unexpected. He always kept his idea of his enemies moved by thinking what he would do in a situation. As his grip tightened on Precious under his coat, he watched the slow crawl of the van as it made its way up the street. It seemed like it was trying to find a lone address, but all the houses on that street had been occupied for awhile and most had vinyl siding. No need for a paint job. What they were trying to find was a target and Solo wasn't trying to be one.

Solo slowly backed up pushing Diamond behind him, like a lion guarding his den. His actions were soon recognized and the van picked up speed just as the side door slid open. When he saw the guns he was hoping two things.

That he wasn't the only one seeing this go down and that he was the only one holding. These were the only thoughts he had time to have as he pushed Diamond and his coat to the ground.

If you would've seen the movements he made, as he let Precious trade words with those in the van, you would've thought he was caught in the Matrix.

Leaning back he got to see one of his shots hit one of the people in the van. And he thought, 'These Niggas can't even shoot'. At the same time it was like he jinxed himself, because not all of the bullets whizzed by him. Falling over the still sprawled body of Diamond from the impact of the bullets, he felt that his time had come too early, too soon.

At first he didn't feel pain from the burning bullets that had entered his body. But when he did, he couldn't tell you where he was shot at, because it hurt allover. The ache kept him from seeing the van crash with all of its occupants dead from the Sangres who had reacted to the obvious commotion going on outside.

He did feel Diamond come from under him sobbing as soon as she seen the blood exiting his wounds.

"No, no," Diamond said cradling Solo's head.

"The...they got me huh?" he breathed.

"Shh...save your energy. It's gonna be okay," she said trying to soothe him. Being a nurse she was supposed to be used to seeing things like this. But she never came across someone this close or important to her. Someone she truly loved.

She did have enough composure to call for an ambulance. And through a flood of tears, she explained what happened, where they were, and who she was, hoping that that would speed their response up, for she was a well-respected and known nurse. She continued to rock Solo, as she coaxed him to be quiet and save his strength to hold on everything was gonna be okay.

But Solo, staring up at Diamond through blurry eyes, could feel himself going and didn't want to leave without saying how he felt. "N- no, no matter what. R-remember. I love you", he said closing his eyes. "Arr," he moaned from the pain.

"Don't, hold on" Diamond said starting to get up. She ran to the Denali and pulled it up on the curb next to Solo. She had some people help put him in the back, then sped off.

"Please, baby don't die. I need you. Please," She recited over and over again as she weaved through traffic. She even ran stop signs and red lights like she was an ambulance herself. She prayed to God no one got in the way, nor someone crossing because she knew that she'd run them over. But that was not to be as she safely made it to the hospital and parked in the same place that EMS would. The people that helped put Solo in the back, had come with her and she had them carry him through the emergency doors.

Already knowing what to be done she ran behind the call desk and paged for a doctor to ban open operating room. A gurney and some assistance came with an IV and took Solo to a surgery room. Diamond quickly ran to where her things were in a locker and changed clothes.

After she scrubbed up she went to where they took Solo. She was semi-relieved to see they had already began normal procedures. She went to the head of the table and looked down at the face of Solo. Her heart was beating so hard and fast that she didn't know what to do, but she knew one thing that she wasn't going nowhere till this was over.

She saw Solo's fluttering eyes as the morphine started to take effect. "It's gonna be alright now," she said running her gloved hand over his head. And watching him she saw his lips move saying something. Leaning down till her ear was an inch from his mouth she heard him.

"It's neva gonna end. But this game is over," came the whispered words out of his mouth. She didn't understand a word that he said, even though she heard him quite clear. But that was the last thing she was worried about as she slipped into unconsciousness.

PART III - CHECKMATE: GAME OVER

CHAPTER 23

It had took quite a while before the once famous store was reopened. There were more renovations to be done than thought; but Hue and his helpers had done a good job you could say it was more than good, because they had done way more than what they were getting paid for. The rehab center was up the street next to an after-school academic program building, for those who needed extra help in their studies. It was almost like a big brother/sister program except better. Because even though you had mentors they were people who the kids could relate to, like rising basketball or football stars from the many colleges in Greensboro. Mainly A&T and Bennet. Two historical Black Colleges you also had aspiring music artist and comedians. These were people the kids looked up to, but had also wormed their way out of the street life.

You had people like Diamond and Cross, who now was owner of three stores and a six-figure man, teaching them about professional life and entrepreneurship. The kids who thought they were hard and street, took to them more easily because they knew what they represented. And listening to them let them know that being gangster wasn't about how you dressed or if you'd bust your gun.

It was about your attitude and how you carried yourself. You had to give to get. Respect to get respected. It wasn't about the violence you saw on TV or read in the newspaper, because that's what the media wanted you to think. There was nothing wrong with wanting to be that doctor, that lawyer, CEO of this or that, and still rep. Being gangsta didn't mean being ignorant or stupid. It meant providing and taking care of your family and loving one another. And by getting that education doors will open up for you, so you don't have to worry about the man locking you up for an unnecessary crime.

The program was a good thing and it turned a lot of people and even though some said it wouldn't last, that it was only because of the entertainment that the people came. But there was a great improvement in the grades of those who attended the program compared to those who didn't. Then there was the rehab center. People also talked bad about thinking it wouldn't work because of where it was situated. But what Hue said rang true. They wanted help, but no one would give it to them. Knowing that in order to buy a piece of crack you had to pass the center made it hard. Especially with people encouraging you to come in. It was like a slap in the face to get help then go back out there and put yourself back where you were.

The center wasn't just a rehab program, it was also a job placement agency. So that recovering addicts had a true fresh start. It didn't take long before people started trickling through the door. Hue being the first person there and new was receiving building contracts from various companies. It didn't sit well with most people, but those amongst the Sangre understood that it was for the better of the oppressed people.

The black dollar that was being used for drugs, made its way back into the community and this was only the beginning. More businesses were going to be erected. That meant more jobs and less people on the streets, their people anyway. Just then a gold suburban pulled up in front of the store. People had seen it roll up and down the street before, but the president tinted windows had kept anyone from getting a glimpse of its passengers. It could've been the police for all they knew, since that's what a lot of them were driving now.

When the driver's side door opened, the person dressed in the forest green wind breaker suit was easily recognized as Diamond. The backdoor was then opened to help out a little boy. It was Shahran Tyrone Divine. Diamond and Solo's son, who had just turned three. Going to the other side, she pulled out an 18- month old, Gloria Divine, who was dressed identical to her mother. When the front passenger side opened no one knew who would step out of the vehicle. The first thing that revealed itself was a gold headed cane followed by an all white Air Force One. The white break away pants was a green stripe going up its side, was matched by an Antwan Walker Boston Celtic throwback and jacket. The green do rag and Celtic fitted hat sat on top of the head of someone who couldn't be easily forgotten.

Solo stood looking at the people gathered on the sidewalk. It had been three years since he was released from the hospital after being shot. He was never expected to make it from all the blood loss and internal damage that was done. But he had survived after losing some of his intestine and he right kidney. A bullet had cracked his kneecap, which was held together with pins, the reason he needed the cane.

The rest of the bullets had either passed through him or were able to be removed. Nothing, he was grateful, was still lodged in him.

He was here to see the opening of his store and be seen after such a long absence. He felt like the Mayor of the eastside. He was greeted with a lot of cheers, smiles and handshakes. When a medium built lady walked up and hugged and kissed him in the cheek, he looked quizzically at Diamond. When she just smiled he looked more closely at the lady and recognition crossed his face, "Sarah?"

"Yup, it's me. How I look?" she asked twirling around.

"Damn! You look good, what happened?" he asked not believing how much she had changed from the skinny fiend he knew. She now stood in front of him in a pair of jeans that hugged her thick thighs and plump backside.

"I stopped smokin'"

"Dat's good. I'm proud of you. But if it wasn't for you I probably couldn't had done this," he said pointing at the three buildings.

"Well, I was good at what I did. But I'm tryin' to put dat behind me and move on."
"Aight. Are you aight? You working or what?"

"I'm lookin', but you know how it is. But I'm aight. I'm stayin' wit a friend till I get it together."

"Fuck dat, I just bought a row of apartments on Gillespie, you can move in one of dem. I'll give you da first month free and I got a friend looking for a secretary. Can you handle dat?"

"Thank you Solo. You've always been good to me. How will I even be able to repay you?"

"Stay straight and don't lose your job. Here call this number, when you're ready to move and be at this address Monday morning at eight o'clock sharp."

"Thank you," she said leaving him the same way that she greeted him.

He turned to Diamond "Where's Cross. I need to talk to him."

"I'll call him."

"Come here Sha," he called to his son who had started to wander. He was dressed just like his father except he was wearing forest like his mother and sister.

Later after the opening of the store, that was just like any other corner store that sold everything from food, clothes and cell phones. Only this store was black owned. Solo was sitting in the back office when Cross was let in by Diamond.

"Sit down."

"You lookin good man."

"I'm feelin' a lot betta than befo."

"So what's up?"

"I'm a point black tell ya. I'm ready to retire."

"Retire?"

"Yeah, retire. I can't do it no more. You see my condition. I can't put in no more work like I use to."

"So what does this have to do with me?"

"I need or should I say, I want you to take over. If I wasn't like this I wouldn't have come to you like this, but I can't keep up wit everybody anymore."

"What about Kase or Chaos?"

"Their mind wouldn't be into it. They street warriors, cat's da only place they ca lead successfully at. I need someone who can carry da weight of both worlds. This is why I taught you all dat I knew so you could one day take over."

"So you layin' ya flag down?"

"Hells nah. Neva dat. If I'm really needed I'll be there. Just consider it like me being da owner and you're da general manager or more live da vice president of da crew."

"I see."

"I'll still work this side of town, develop a few more things. You'll see about buildin' up da otha three sides. I want our imprint on everything. Keep it in da family. I know what you did wit dem stores you run and I expect nothin' less. After we get things going here, we'll reach out to different cities, then states. But dat's still a long way off. Do you think this can be done?"

"Wit da right financial backin' yeah."

"Then you accept my offer?"

"Have I ever turned you down?" Cross smirked.

"No, but I don't wanna force nothin on you."

"You can't force me to nothing' dats for da cause. Dat's what I live for as you've taught me."

"Good. 'cause there's a lot to be done. This is da beginning of a new era. This is what being a Sangre is about. But remember," he said remembering Hue's words. "This a different world I'm trying to conquer, not as easy as da streets. But you already know dat don't you?" he said getting up and preparing to leave.

"Yeah, it's very different." Cross answered following Solo out of the office.

"But dat's why I chose you," he said before telling Diamond, who was behind the counter with one of the Sangres showing him what to do, that he was headed up the street.

"I know you can handle it. Plus, we got enough people, who are business minded, at your disposal. Along with me and Diamond. Where's to go but up." He continued as they walked through the door and headed towards the rehab center.

"Whenever you're ready to start, I'm a need to know what we're working' wit and where we have to start to get where we wanna go."

"Not a problem, but where we start is right here and I already told you where I'm tryin to take it. I want our name in people's mouths like Johnson and Johnson, and Microsoft."

"That's a lot."

"I'm not gonna think small. If they can do it, why not us?"

"And what do plan on callin' this enterprise you seek to build?

"Not seek. I am. And it's gonna be called R.I.P.P. Rest In Peace Pinero after our lost friend."

Cross nodded in agreement as they entered the rehab center. It was a reasonable name. So that their friend and brother's name was remembered whenever you came across one of their present and future business.

Diamond hated to let Solo out of her sight. She quickly went to the door and watched as he and Cross made their way up the street. She could hear parts of their conversation and it dawned on her what he had said on his death bed.

"It's neva gonna end. But this game was ova."

She knew of his fascination of Chess, but didn't realize that he compared it to life till one night he spoke to her about it. The pain and suffering never stopped but each game had to be played differently. He had won his street match, but at the time, almost lost in the end.

What would be the outcome of this match up? A professional mind was more dangerous than a street person's mentality. The street person would kill you whenever he could all by himself. The professional would get someone to do it for them, while keeping their hands clean. At the same time, they'd did it only if you were threatening competition. Either way Diamond knew that Solo was about to run into a whole different type of animal and she'd be by his side every step of the way.

ABOUT THE AUTHOR

Lex was born on Nov. 2,1979 to Mr. and Mrs. Day in Boston (Dorchester), Massachusetts. He later moved to Tampa, Florida, then Orangeburg, South Carolina, and finally to Greensboro, North Carolina. It was in Greensboro that he ran into some trouble, landing him in prison for six years.

After reading countless urban novels, Lex found his craft for literature and being able to formulate a story of his own. It wasn't until serving another stint for 12 years that he became serious about his craft.

Even though this is his first published novel, he has penned 13 to date, bringing real life situations to fictional readers.

ORDER MORE BOOKS

www.TheSolidFoundationGroup.com

Book	
	CheckMate: It's Your Move by Lex *Genre: Urban* *Cost: $15.95/each**
	A Portrait of Virginia A. Smith by Virginia A. Smith *Genre: Biography / Inspirational* *Cost: $13.95/each**
	Poetic Motifs' Significance of 9 *by Kish Andes* *Genre: Poetry* *Cost: $13.95/each**
	How To Fade Like Griffin *by Kendrick Henderson* *Genre: Educational* *Cost: $15.95/each**
	The Pig Who Became President *By Alana Johnson* *Genre: Children's* *Cost: $12.95/each**
	Set Free by Truth *By Amari Johnson* *Genre: Children's* *Cost: $12.95/each**
	Bullet Proof *by Bodie Quinette* *Genre: Self-Help / Motivational* *Cost: $15.95/each**
	The Cartel's Daughter Unedited: Raw and Uncut! *by Carmine* *Genre: Crime / Thriller / Urban* *Cost: $14.99/each**